I0589084

The Case Of Aleister Stratton
Compiled by K.G.V. Barnwell

G
Grosvenor Artist Management

Of course it was the spelling of the name Aleister Stratton that attracted my attention to this book. The name itself isn't unusual but the strange spelling was of interest to me. The only other time I had seen the name Aleister was indeed here in Hastings, a town I had come to live in and a place from which many remarkable coincidences of my life seemed to stem. Until I moved here from a past in central London I held a somewhat circumspect view of natural coincidence.

Aleister Crowley, the self-styled most evil man in England and an occultist, had lived out his final days in Hastings. Visiting the History House I learnt how, dressed in his signature black fedora and cloak, he haunted the bookshops of the Old Town. His presence caused a heavy psychological pall to hang over anywhere he frequented, leaving the physicality of the devil and unspoken Faustian pacts in his wake.

To read the name Aleister in this very book, on the shelves of the Albion bookshop, automatically sent shivers down my spine. The name, once again in my path, now with the surname of Stratton, would turn out to be an equally disturbing story.

The book I held would become a personal voyage weaving a thread of fact and fiction through my sceptical and chary mind.

I scarcely know where to begin or end. How to make sense of the passages I have read. I shudder at the close reality of events and at all the possibilities of this story being a rare case of surprising truths.

P.W.

First published in 2016 by

Grosvenor Artist Management
32/32 Grosvenor Street
Mayfair
London
W1K 4QS
www.grosvenorartistmanagement.com

ISBN 978-0-9574980-6-8

'Here we are all, by day;
by night we are hurled

By dreams, each one
into a several world.'

Robert Herrick (1591-1674)

Part I

There were rumblings of discontent abroad. This was a somewhat unconventional occurrence, emanating as it did from the depths of the normally scholastic somnolence of Professor Holland's study. The constant need to reach to the highest shelves in the library had stretched the Professor's already tall, lean frame. The crescent shape of his posture, imposed on him by the need to peruse and correct the work of his pupils at their desks, presently uncurled itself from a pile of dusty history papers. He sighed like a deflated balloon.

The Professor was the most popular and most approachable of teachers, as agreed by pupils and staff alike. To witness his appearance that early afternoon, one would find him uncharacteristically cross.

Often at this time of day he enjoyed imbibing a little of his personal collection of finest Madeira, which could be assured of bringing the brightest of pink highlights to his cheeks. Today was different. This morning his eye had been caught by a concisely written piece, cramped and almost hidden at the foot of the newspaper's obituary page; a section to which he turned daily. It read:

'17th April 1992, the recently discovered body and unexplained death of a

London born man, Aleister Stratton.'

The Professor prided himself on his clear-headed ability to recall names and facts. The name was familiar to him, yet irritatingly unavailable for immediate mental retrieval. Thus, he held, for some period, a disgruntled and distracted demeanour; the deep concentration accentuating the small furrow in his brow. For minutes beyond his marking, his extreme annoyance over this perplexing and enticing surfacing of something as simple as *'a name,'* became the total embodiment of his focus. He tapped his fingers rhythmically, rolled his eyes about the room, hoping to strike an angle for an answer, whilst simultaneously filing through his selective memory.

Professor Harold Richard Holland knew he had to write a book; he was a leading authority on the Fine and Decorative Arts, as yet though, an unpublished one. Three years ago his adoring and endlessly patient wife had expensively compiled a fine album with his initials embossed in gold on the wide spine: HRH. How often he had applauded his parents' choice of names for their son. However the album awaited the prose and perceptions of his life's work; to be finally ascribed the seriousness of pen to paper and thence to publication. Daily the Professor heard the quiet whispers of indignation from the refined leaves of the empty book, nudging his reluctant brain into applying its well taught self.

'When will you start to form sentences and begin a triumphal epic?

What if I got stuck and could not proceed? It would be worse than before; an unfinished writer, capable of readings and criticisms but not of my own originality. The shame of it! The humiliation!'

The gentle but continuous rain ran in rivulets down the individual panes of thin, delicate Georgian glass. He looked out onto the square below, watching people dart about; the odd flash of colour catching his eye; a red scarf, a striped umbrella. Before long the drains would block and the pipes would overflow. Frantic streams of escaping water would run across the paving, desperate to find some uncluttered gutter in which to pass their deluge. He could predict the pattern; this was, after all, his window onto the world.

With the distant sound of the university clock striking the quarter hour he was instantly returned to his younger, more dare devil days when he experimented with life as a student in the dramatic and blackened baroque city of

Dresden. The sound of the bell in the clock at the Zwinger museum shaping his days into quarterly segments; where, when idle, his fascinated youth sought stimulus from every direction.

Today's newspaper and its rather oblique reference to *'the unexplained death of Aleister Stratton'* had pushed aside the normal timetable tidiness of the Professor's day and sent him clumsily seeking clues to raise Mr Stratton up into relevance. The thought of his death as *'unexplained'* was not the laboured point of his eager and desperate search, but merely the burning sensation of a familiar, if un-placeable set of two words that made up *Aleister Stratton.* In even smaller print, beneath the announcement, was a solemn, standard appeal for information and a local London police number. The police clearly required the help of the general public in what was evidently, an unusual discovery.

Several precious hours had been wasted starting at the bottom of his study and working up through his shelves. Finally the Professor succumbed to weariness and flopped into his elderly chair; it was, like his study, inherited from his predecessor Professor Giles. From his seated position Holland enjoyed his daily appreciation of the glorious Royal Park. His graceful window shaded by a perfect English climbing rose gave on to a vista of timeless elegance; the poor plant now bedraggled and soaked; the view, simply bleak and grey if traceable at all. Designed by nineteenth century landscape gardeners the sight afforded from his room had remained largely unchanged for over one hundred years. He thought of the 400 rose varieties set in their beds, recalling the early summer walks of heady floral perfumes and the pillow-soft petals, dusting his nose in pollen specks. This seasonal outlook gave him mental peace; a remedy regularly founded in nature and its elements. With a sudden unforeseen break in one of the deepest and heaviest clouds, he too found a shaft of light: *'Of course!'*

Twenty years ago the Professor had arrived at the university with the fresh enthusiasm of a newly recruited member of the faculty. He had been overwhelmed, and rather nervous of his new position; most intriguingly though he had become the beneficiary of three books; books belonging to the previous incumbent of this study. He had learnt little of the man, except his name, Giles, an English Literature enthusiast and who, after an outwardly comfortable career, had passed away peacefully in retirement. A photo of him hung in the assembly hall along with previous scholars and alumni. There was nothing striking or distinctive about him, an ordinary man with a passion for books. The dishevelled young boys blended into a carbon background, book-ended by their masters and their names barely legible from sun scars.

Professor Holland returned in his mind to those benefactors long ago who gave all new professorial arrivals these books: The Bible, a set of The Encyclopaedia Britannica and The Collins English Dictionary. He leapt to his slightly over-large feet and grabbing a highly unreliable side table to stand on, stretched his arms to the top shelf; they would supply the answer.

The table, unused to the insult of being expected to withstand the weight of a human being, promptly gave way. The disregard for the poor lamp was totally out of character but epitomised the theme of the morning. The Professor and the dictionary, for which he was aiming, tumbled in a rather ungainly manner to the floor, followed by a cascade of handwritten sheets of paper. With a brief loss of composure, the Professor regained his stature, sat at his desk and re-ordered the ageing and fingered papers.

There was the name he had first seen so long ago on papers clipped inside this book. At that point in time he had let it pass, dealing with his own affairs was a time consuming task, but now he needed to understand. He had not consulted the old dictionary before because he did, of course, have his own treasured copy with scribbles in the margins and folded edges. Now a man, *Aleister Stratton,* was dead, and the word he had at first overlooked, *'unexplained'* began to float into focus. The details of his death were sparse and non explicit; the police were holding something back and needed answers. With a tinge of trepidation, which often comes with taking a foreign holiday when one wonders what you are letting yourself in for, Professor Holland took up the notes. He read the firm and bold hand: *Herewith I give you my account of The Case of Aleister Stratton by his teacher, Professor Giles.*

Part II

I, Professor Giles, shall begin with my part in the strange mystery, in which I have become entangled. I must remark I make no wish of being drawn into baffling adventures. I am a simple man of means and pleasures. I prefer facts to fiction and answers to questions; for most days I deal with fictional stories in lessons. In life there must be truth, and a satisfactory explanation for everything, if we are to believe what is said to us. All religions have a book which forms the basis of their beliefs. The passages and stories are read and re-read; their discrepancies and variations lie between us all. Daily we are dictated to by routine and fashion, by probability, by factors and circumstances. Every beginning must end and every start must finish, and we shall exist in forms of opposites or in the gradations of opposites. If my mood is happy, its opposite may be sad and these are extremes, like the contrasts of black and white. However I may exist in the moods of less abrupt meaning, to feel fine or pensive for example. Colours live in groups or pools with many layers: cream in white or pink in red. I am not a man of great philosophy or thinking and I cannot spend my days dwelling on what I cannot see; we have doctors for all manner of issues. My sister is a doctor. She spends her time studying the mind, observing habits, listening to the cerebral turmoil of humanity whether individuals walk into her practice or through the advantages of eavesdropping.

'The mind is a morass of complications and unpredictability' she would often respond, whether you had asked for a synopsis or whether you had not.

It is almost certain my sister, I shall introduce her here, Doctor Nottingham, taking her husband's name, would find herself repeating this very phrase several times a day. In retrospect I find it quite sinister and it would not be long before I would be challenging her with a puzzling case. If I digress you must forgive me. It is likely I may wander from time to time to elaborate the story or case that I present to you with my own asides. I am learning as I write how situations develop; how when you live them they appear one way, yet when written there is a chance for your thoughts to flow independently. However I have been a Professor for nigh on 25 years and the incident which befell me the day Aleister Stratton walked into my study is sure to outwit and surprise the most learned of men and women.

I cannot recall in great detail the day of this boy's arrival. He was rather quiet and unassuming with better recommendations than demonstration. Perhaps it is unfair to assume that a boy of 24 could slip easily into the companionship of others in the final year of study. Boys are usually great comrades in the classroom with a healthy sense of competitiveness. Aleister Stratton had made a very sensitive first impression and as a place of high learning we do value the health and welfare of our students. In my view it is always important to leave your study door open and to be as generous with your time to students as possible. Perhaps that is why he came to knock mildly at my door, some time into the first term. I admit I was surprised. It must have taken great courage and deliberation to walk the carpeted and creaky steps up to my room. A route mostly reserved for boys faltering in their performance, and who needed guidance and some refining of academic discipline with extra tutorial studies. Stratton showed great promise if a little reticent to participate in class discussions. His weekly essays on English Literature topics were well reasoned and presented with thoroughly convincing deliberations.

It was late on a Friday when he came searching

me out; Mrs Lewis, my secretary, had left half an hour before. This remains clear to me as the five o'clock bell on a Friday heralds the start of the weekend: the students become twitchy and eager to close book and Mrs Lewis always has social arrangements planned. Very quickly the college rooms and teacher studies are hollowed out; there is the tender humming of pipes and of water swirling around the iron radiator units like gurgling giants, before shutting off completely and dying their bodies' cold.

I welcomed him kindly, speaking before the boy had even turned or raised his head. He seemed dispirited and disillusioned, so lacking the natural vigour and vibrancy of many of these boys, yet I would have said this was in no way out of character. It took much to raise the solemn child at the best of times and I felt sorry that he should be wasting his youth with an age soaked demeanour.

"Aleister, take a seat," I said indicating a tall, cushioned chair.

He placed his hands on the slatted frame, rocked it to and fro, and then took two steps towards the window instead, as if he could not settle for comfort, and felt easier with his awkwardness. His eyes moved to some middle distance.

"Something you're missing?" I continued, perhaps asking a question might urge him to move into

conversation. Although if this was to be a series of monosyllabic responses, where I dug for potential questions, in hope of finally striking lucky with his train of thought and waking his mind up into some string of intelligence, I was not in the mood, not on a Friday night.

He maintained an air of elusiveness, which many would have mistaken for arrogance, but not in Aleister. I may have known little of him, but I would not brand an unusual boy with such a harsh term. In fact his disposition held more questions than answers and it's unlikely he would be able to answer for them. I had done all my weekly pupil appraisals and was really ready to retire home, so in waiting for him to make the next move, I decided to reorganise a few books.

"It's a long way up here," he coughed, *"you'd break your neck if you fell."*

Aleister moved back to the chair, sat down, straightened his back, and lifted his head. I mirrored his actions so we were now face on in height.

"How can I help you young man?" I tried, although nothing could have prepared me, or anyone, for such a direct answer.

"Sir," he spoke softly, *"I...I have committed two murders, my sister and my mother...they are both dead...now you must think me terrible."*

I recoiled, sucking at air suddenly devoid of

oxygen; a soundless reaction to shock. He looked me in the eye deadly serious. I pictured fear rise into his dilating pupils; dark and expansive until all recognition of colour disappeared. The hypnotic stare smothered my attention. I almost forgot his prior statement, until I fell back into my chair, into a realm of my own sense and situation. Perhaps my reaction was just as he had expected, maybe he had practised this very meeting all day, within the confines of his head. I assessed Aleister's pose, he now possessed an unnatural calm. Who was this boy, this quiet-confessing student? Academically he found the lessons no doubt dull, sitting through the classes with the affliction of easy genius. I found no mockery in this self assurance: a bright child will always suffer this way.

I was a Professor, I had responsibility and position, if he speaks so plainly, then I will let him lead, and leave my impulses to nature. If this was some boyish jest, some comical escapade, some dare-devil to cast me as a fool, Aleister was the least likely of originators. The musky room had cooled and the daylight was dimming to a hazy, blurry light of smudged charcoal. I watched as Aleister moved back to the doorway. He was calm; there was not one disturbed feature or abnormality about his persona, no thin veil of disguise under which he hid. He was as he always seemed. He did not revolt me or cling to some desperate plea for clemency and pity. He did not search me, and I accepted the resolute manner and charming young face as I might have accepted a ticket to the theatre.

Feeling my inquiring conscience build to speculation; *'a crescendo of curious extremes'* would have been Doctor Nottingham's analysis. She was both resolute and romantic. Then thoughts, never before considered as I had never prepared for such a revelation, flooded my head. Why, what would become of this? Could this boy be a risk? Are there other violent undisclosed secrecies? Now I was the one who shared the burden. Is there trouble in a melancholy boy that renders him neither desperately low nor exceedingly high, so he may not be stirred or affected by anything? Is he any of these things or am I simply suffering from *'a heat oppressive brain.'* Although I quote from the fictional work of *'Macbeth,'* I am a factual man, much of what we believe to be fiction is so closely based on fact that at some point, somewhere, for someone, the two words swop: one writer's fiction is another man's reality. I admit I felt heat in the palm of my hands and forehead; a tingle of sweat. I was no accomplice to the murder, yet I was tainted with the knowledge of it. I was now in some way involved. How did this happen? I cannot undo what has been said. I cannot un-know what I have heard. I cannot let it sit either. In short, I am part of what happens next. Before my musings became any freer, he said clearly, *"I want to show you what I've done. I want you to see."* This was an invitation to depart. I followed in his wake, down the stairs, over the well-worn carpets; the steps creaking under the weight of our alternate footfall.

'After sunset tonight, I will know more, and much of it I may not like.' I said to myself.

In the shadows of the porch-way, I caught a glimpse of the sunset. I had been desperately seeking something natural, beautiful and soul-warming as we descended the stairwell.

The heavy, dark-centred clouds slowly closed over the bleeding orange sun, like the healing of a wound, only soon it would be dark and I already felt myself punched of life.

Part III

By the time we completed our descent into town, trailing several steps behind Aleister as I was, the lamp posts were in full flood. It was difficult to keep up with him; the streets were crowded in silvery silhouettes. His shoes had a distinctive click as we moved over the pavement and I focused more on their sound, keeping my head low and my thoughts loose. We passed through many of the busy squares of London, some people ending their days and some beginning their evenings and each passing by with directed pace like moveable pawns in the game of life. It was a thick, smoky cold night; breaths of air were sharp and scratchy on the throat. I found it easier to cough quietly for air rather than heave a deep breath to receive it. I drew little attention to myself as other pedestrians seemed to apply the same technique. I remember spotting someone I knew, a good, loyal friend, Mr Tomlin, a bridge partner and excellent sportsman, cricket was his game. We had played a rubber together only last week and now here I was embroiled in such disorder. I hoped, *'Dear God'* he would not pounce on me. I felt guilty for bowing my head so low, walking in a determined and concealed manner, speeding up as I approached him and relaxing my shoulders only as we moved further from his sight until he was well out of range of recognition. Aleister never once looked to see if I was close, perhaps he held some intuition, knowing I would follow, knowing I could not resist a chase through London. In truth I started to tire, the wind picked up, harassing my hat and coat, upsetting my equilibrium. Suddenly I wanted to be at home, safe inside a warm house with the anticipation of a home cooked meal and soft slippers. For the first time in what must have been a speedy 20 minute walk, Aleister turned to me, waited for me to catch up and said simply, *"we are just across there,"* gesturing his hands in an unhelpful way. I was cross, but he wouldn't understand, *"let's end this"* I said abruptly, keen he should take the hint. Then I remembered why I was here, *'what was I about to witness?'* All the heat drained from my body, I shivered. He motioned us to a long park bench. It was fixed outside a locked, private garden square which was surrounded by traditional cast-iron spiked railings. I took particular interest in their form. At the base was an intricate, intertwining leaf and flower design; an arabesque curvilinear decoration which, for one long second, filled my mind with a small absurd distraction. It seems trivialities would jump in and out of my mind all evening, perhaps it was a useful mechanism for dealing with the threat of tonight's theatrical performance. This square was not its usual secretive, luxurious green but a deep expanse of black. I leapt at the chance of a firm, smooth seat; both my feet and mind ached in united sympathy for each other. How I missed the pleasures of the indoors and the peace of my own home. How every night, with few exceptions, I enjoyed the same calm routine, my pattern of many years, until tonight's disruptive expedition. For someone like my sister this would have been a great adventure, studying the mind and manner of this man. For me, this was not the case, yet I know she will have me repeating the unravelling exploits in minute detail, to her inquisitive mind full of theories. This evening would represent an eruption of untapped ideas. She would claim her clinical studies required the content, although I knew how much she loved to analyse the actions of people. I would happily have exchanged places with her, but the matter lay with me. I shall stick to my wits, follow what is presented to me and with hindsight present this whole set of events to her. The outcome was out of my control.

I sat there for two, maybe three minutes, before I sensed Aleister was not with me. Leaning back in the direction I had unswervingly walked, I noticed him talking nonchalantly to a petite, young woman with bunched chestnut-brown hair. Her face was plain and wide and her features so small, as if they'd been sketched and left unfinished by a portraitist. Such an ease of manner I could not have anticipated; an observation I would make numerous times over the course of the evening. Only a few minutes ago we were pacing across London, and now here he was with the rehearsed airs and graces of an Oxbridge squire, as if his days were filled with leisurely hours, as if his time was for informal pleasantries and polite dalliances. Quite the charmer, but then tonight of all nights, he needed to be. I dwelt on this change of appearance and summed it up thus: when men feel their most guilty or most watched, they present an overly interested and attentive persona, such as all soft faced, mellow females' desire. Conversely were they rude or unpleasant their behaviour would alert a conscious alarm. To me Aleister was totally out of character; a sign that he'd acted in some false image to pacify the unexpected and startling meeting of a figure he obviously knew. His sickly sweetness towards a society he despised, doused the scene in an atmosphere of forthcoming doom. A doom and devastation he would present to me, and thus plague my memory and reflections.

He spotted me staring blankly; I must have looked rather lost and confused. I felt like a forgotten dog whose owner had suddenly found a more interesting companion. My look convinced him *I* must now take precedent. When the young lady was waved off he strolled towards the bench and finally took his position beside me. We covered the bench preventing passersby from making it their nightly perch. The waxy moon was full and curving, blotted with grey patches, as deep as maroon bruises. It was a remarkably crisp, black sky. The injured moon fought to expose the sins of the night and cast a light on our clandestine mission. How I wished for a plain, ordinary evening. Days I could write up in my diary as simple, sensible and serene; nights I could write in my sleep, almost printed before I awoke.

What a confounded mess! What had made me follow this unconventional path? I was helpless and worst of all quite beyond my depth of liking.

Part IV

"That house is mine." Aleister said, pointing to a large, perfectly proportioned Victorian villa, with four Portland-stone steps, flanked by two slender columns and a protective portico front entrance. It was on a wide corner; the profile long and deep.

"I live here with my mother and sister. My father died 15 years ago and my brother lives in the city. But," he paused for effect, *"my sister and mother are now dead and I'll live alone."*

"You say all this in such a matter of fact fashion," I tested him.

"Well it is a fact," he said, *"there are no lights on, don't you think that's odd in a house occupied by women?"*

"It cannot be odd if you tell me they are dead." I reasoned.

"Yes, and that's why I brought you here, to the scene of my crime, I'm not running you see, I'm calm, look at me."

He did not turn his head as you might expect but I excused him, for the light was dim, as if we were clothed in sepia brown or photographed using poor quality film. I made no quick judgement despite the coarseness of his attitude. This short, whispery conversation between us would have seemed somewhat conspiratorial to any onlooker should he have spied our self-conscious body language and tight, staccato movement of the mouth.

Then, as if to lighten the mood, since we could not brighten the lamps, Aleister offered me a toffee. A toffee, I ask you! This was not a theatre interval or even the prelude; he was un-wrapping a sweet. Perhaps an apple of sin would have been more appropriate, and then I thought of the poisoned apple in fairy tales. What injury the apple has incurred! He twisted and creased the wrapper in an irritating, continuous, fixated manner. Funny how you recall the little things. In fact it abruptly reminded me of an incident weeks ago when I spotted Aleister at lunch in the university canteen. It struck me as peculiar to watch the boy eating his bread roll; he stabbed it carelessly with a knife, scooped out the inside dough, put the soft crumb in his pocket and continued to chew the crust in small morsels; with the butter, he took a portion and with the remainder he just squashed it; the thumb inflicting the carnage. It was unsightly, but he was oblivious to me or any other being. It is what my sister would call, *'obsessive behaviour.'* It is all very well with bread and butter, but has this led on to greater things? It's queer how the mind works, after the one little scenario I wondered mostly what might become of the spongy dough he was collecting inside his pocket – he didn't seem like the duck-feeding type. I had thought little of it until this eventful minute.

Of course I did not accept the toffee; how stupid it would seem at the inquest of my death, the doctor reading, *'he accepted a sweet from a man who was a self confessed murderer,'* the lowering tone and insinuation inclining to, *'what were you thinking, fool.'*

"No, thanks," I said, and then thrust forward with my voice as if directed by an invisible conductor's baton into a duet song, *"Aleister, why don't you tell me what's really going on? The truth, however you want to present it to me, I'm here to listen."* And to myself, *'I've come this far, just on the whim of your statement. Speak, before I change my mind, and the desire for a strong drink and the soreness from my feet override your creepy, night-time stories.'*

I also began to add new characters into my thoughts who would love a tale or two to share; the interests of my sister and her studies into the sometimes malevolent workings of the human brain. There was my son of similar age, who now lives abroad. I hope that if he came to any trouble, there would be the sympathetic ear of a trusted man or woman, willing to give him time and patience. Mr Tomlin, as fore-mentioned, told me only two weeks ago that I was, and he put this kindly, *'all too set in my ways and means.'* Perhaps I *should* have let him witness the chase through London's web of streets at an odd hour, tight on the heels of an adventure. My wife too, spoke of how she hoped we could get away from the city sometime soon, to stir our heads with some seaside air. A story such as this would surely be a breath of many salty waters to the chest! Thus I would forego the numbness in my ankle, iron out the frown upon my forehead, and sit with the composure of a cat and the tolerance of the teacher I was.

In accordance with Aleister's methods, this house had now become the scene of a crime. I found he needed no more coercion. He spoke freely, frankly and never once faltered. He had perfected the art of soliloquies: I was beside him no more. I remained a perfunctory, like the bench; as indiscernible as the breath of oxygen charging his spirit.

The following passage is Aleister's story: recounted by him after the hideous affair took place, *'I have committed two terrible murders, my sister and my mother.'* It is word for word the story he related to me that evening we sat together on the cold, dank seat.

He handed it to me to read, *'at leisure,'* he said, as if I might enjoy the recommendation of a best-selling book.

Part V

The murders recorded by Aleister Stratton

I have never cared that much for people. In my life they have all too frequently let me down, and without sounding old before my time, I have come to rely entirely upon myself. It is the safest means; who better to trust than yourself? By opening your heart and mind to someone, you expose vulnerability. We cannot taint everybody with the same brush but time and time again, the laughing, the mimicking, the belittling, the insults, the insinuations; they become a tormenting form of verbal bullying, without alternatives you resort inwards. Yes it's true I do live in a family house comprising my sister and mother, but I lead a very separate life from them. The house being so large with many rooms and six different floors, I have passed weeks without seeing any family member, each of us concerned and preoccupied with our own business. I find it comparable to a boarding house; the comings and goings of people, their scent or odd sounds transported through the walls; their drifting shadows like indistinguishable nightly apparitions.

Still I have many interesting daily conversations,

often when I'm out walking or reading; these are held entirely with myself. I have invented a whole table full of people who sit round and discuss whatever topic I choose, sometimes it's just one or two who represent different sides of my personality. It is not something I've ever dwelt on or even found the need to write down, it's just as it is.

'The mind has a thousand eyes,' spoke a poem I once read. No doubt I wear an unusual expression on my face as I wander around the streets of London from one destination to another. My sister once remarked that I lived in *'an Arctic climate'* - distant and unapproachable. If I exude this coldness it is purely the result of the chains of nature. Many of my thoughts debate their stories with each other and of course the facial features bear the brunt of these internal conflicts.

These are, do not think, always arguments or strong testaments, many may be mundane or pedestrian thoughts, like so many practical chats among people. *'Oh the weather!'* *'Oh the queue for the bus!'* *'What to buy for lunch.'* Who can ever know what might be the choice of subject; the day is long and many things can be cast into your path. I was reading a Romantic adventure story once and I know people looked on me strangely as I considered openly (yet to me alone) what the outcome would be for the protagonist of the novel and his foes, the Italian bandits. Would there be a violent vendetta or a clever and deadly negotiation? Would the man ever be able to retrieve the lost years of his life? Would his friends believe it was him after such a long absence? Revenge had made him mad and furious, but still confinement had taught him patience and exactitude. The men he faced would get their come-uppance and he would make sure it was dealt with in such a way that he remained innocent, thereby retaining his pride and honesty without damaging his character which he had fought so hard to preserve and respect. This was my analysis of a fictional book, having saved me from many lonely hours. I had become part of its fabric; to pick it up and begin a new chapter was as exciting and pleasurable as enjoying the company of friends - and challenging, motivating, highly intriguing friends at that!

As to school and coursework, occasionally there are lectures, tours and exhibitions dotted about London or a short train journey from it but mostly I form passages and essays whilst out in the park. I always research topics at the library or in school rooms for thorough understanding. It is good to choose a variety of books published in different decades, particularly with History of Art, whose insight into paintings and sculpture, their provenance and ownership is a forever changing and debatable issue. The fine and very moveable line between a great master and the great master's studio workshop causes endless dispute within the critics' circle. The new discoveries in Art; their consequences and repercussions can make very lively discourse and the shift between what is authentic and genuine to what is parading as false and fraudulent is very sensitive. It appears to me that I have a love of the inanimate. An Old Master painting can hold many secret clues and hidden depths, you just have to be able to read them; what we know of the work, and what we retrieve, makes it all the more valuable, both in substance and in money. In fact Art is a changeable and highly thrilling subject, far more exciting than a fast car or speed boat whose thrill is a shallow, short-lived stunt.

You, who read this, are really waiting to hear of how and perhaps why I murdered the two people who must mean the most to me in the entire world: I have no two such people. The fussiness and fastidiousness, the questioning, and the interfering have led me to clearly believe

I am not a relative of this family. However it is apparent from other irritating relatives, that I greatly resemble my father: an early portrait of him confirms this point.

Well it's true for sure, I am calm and collected yet I had to tell someone of the murders and the only person I had any connection with, in terms of seeing and being near, was Professor Giles. I approached him the day after the incident; murders always take place at night. Does it make them seem more dreadful? Day illuminates the evidence, whereas night shields it, as if encouraging you to commit the deadliest deeds within its company, welcoming you to the dark side. The current winter has provided some of the longest, shrouded evenings on record.

In our complex house of draughty rooms, many of which are unused, there is my dead father's study; he was a medic, a doctor of sorts. I never knew him. I was ten years old when he died. As a child I rarely remember seeing him; he had no affinity with children, least of all me, his third. He had no participation in my upbringing; there was only one time I can call him to mind. It must have been two weeks before his own death; the cause of which I never knew and, in my presence, was never discussed. The obvious pain it brought my mother was enough to produce an eternal silence on the subject. Every evening when I was struggling to get to sleep, (I had bouts of prolonged wakefulness during my childhood) he would say to me, *'Take an element of your life and blend it with imagination. Turn the world your way Aleister.'* That was it, no fairytale, no verse, just an ambiguous sentence to a justifiably confused little boy. I wanted to fly, I wanted a memory of my father, and he gave me these words to contemplate before bed. I repeated them for years; he didn't even make them rhyme.

Please do not pity me, you cannot miss what you did not have and I had no father. When he left us I felt no remorse or bitterness. As I grew older, I got to know him by what he had left within our house including a portrait of himself with a falcon and several stuffed, repulsive animals. They had eyes that followed me around the room, and haunted me for days. He also bequeathed a grand selection of books on medicines, homeopathy, and remedies. I spent time sifting through his cabinets of curiosities, pulling out bottles and labels. This was the best fun he could offer me and with a mind as active and creative as mine, it became my playground;

my refuge and salvation from the boredom of ordinary people and ordinary lives.

Only a few days ago, I opened the door of his study for a mere minute of undiluted interest. In our house it is possible for a room to languish unvisited for years. Why meddle with what is not wanted? On *this* day I felt encouraged to spend some time surrounded by my father's old pieces. The weather was dull and dreary; clouds had settled on the ceiling of the city with only weak, sporadic, pitiful puffs of wind to push them north. An inadequate day of an unpopular month.

I had been to the university lectures I was requested to attend and written the desired essays; their deadline was the Friday. Bored and disillusioned I sought an outlet for my familial frustrations. In the study I came across my weapon: a powder, but not just any powder, a plain white poisonous one. When mixed into a solution of tap water it becomes the neatest, murderous instrument possible - if delivered correctly. I spent the next two hours examining and considering its potential.

The powder, I must tell you, had nothing to do with my father's collection of ointments. This upper area of the house had been plagued by an infestation of rats and the area had been sealed off for some time whilst they were eradicated. In the meantime a sign had directed me so forth, to this substance, the components of which I would use to eliminate my own regrettable connections.

The period passed like an eclipse: steadily, coolly and efficiently; from the hazy dark grey, to which I had become so accustomed, to a situation of soft, sulky light. I had to check myself occasionally, as I felt eyes all around me, watching more in apprehension than judgment. Quite probably it was the arrangement of pinned butterflies and stuffed vermin that disturbed me the most; the sufferance of their deaths displayed everywhere in uneasy triumph. The powdery poison resembled plain bathroom talc; there was plenty to spare, I could afford to experiment liberally. The box instructions and warnings had been worn away, most likely for some time, as to the expiry of the contents, I guessed it to be years old; the risk to a person's health just as deadly. Taking a disused bottle of clear glass I added half a teaspoon, filling the remainder with tap water. All the implements I required were within a hand's distance; measuring spoons, jug, gloves, cloths, a funnel, cork bottle tops, a long stirrer. It was as if everything had been neatly laid out for me, like a proposed surgical procedure. I hadn't just found my source of destruction, it had found me: waiting and ready. Did this make the guilt or prick of conscience the easier to cope with? I never *had* any of these feelings, as far as I was concerned it was a plan well constructed, all I needed to do was to use my own intelligence and initiative to put the exploit into action. I was the precursor and the catalyst. In court, I would present no plausible plea, for no-one could dispute my legitimate reasons for creating death. I have not considered the preservation of my life in the world after this undertaking. All I seem capable of outwardly stating is, I must have been born, unfurnished with conscience. The ultimate goal of finite revenge was far more vigorous and demanding and satisfying than a drop of insipid guilt; my drink was dry.

Over a persistent period in the study, I tried many variations; a larger amount of 'talc' (I so called it) to water until the suspension appeared too cloudy and suspicious. I boiled the water to see if this affected the solution. The talc only dissolved more quickly, leaving fewer residues and oddly, in comparison with the cold solution, which never quite fully dissolved, left minuscule white balls of separated talc to float to the surface like fat globules of whole milk in a hot, weak tea. The precision of this chemistry had to be perfect. Subsequently I decided on a bottle containing two heaped teaspoons of talc to 250ml of not quite boiling water. This solution fully absorbed the powder and prevented the glass bottle from cracking. I could then allow this to cool, and was pleased to present to myself the final potion: I labelled it *'spirits to be.'* As to its flavour – well I wasn't to test it! It would certainly have to be disguised in a strong drink, hiding both its slight cloudy suspension and potentially curious taste. With my mind already progressing to the next stage of this plan, I was sure to overcome each obstacle barring my advance. I poured the substance into a ceramic pot, to see how it would react in a different material. It innocently betrayed the eye, hiding its lethality. The deception would be perfect and I applauded myself in creating a magnificent ruin.

You think I am boasting? I believe myself to be witty when this is lunacy; a crime of the first degree; insanity? I am methodical and directed and I have found my way to a peace that is beyond common sense. This is to be an accomplishment, after years of pent up anguish and family protestations. Perhaps physically I showed signs of weakness and instability, at one point my hands started to shake which made pouring the water and administering the talc onto the spoons somewhat cumbersome. My teeth started to chatter, just as my temperature cooled, but I allowed none of these body deficiencies to hold me back.

Then I put the question to myself and the team of people inside my head: how was I to test this substance? I had worn a tight pair of old gloves, little spillage had taken place despite my involuntary wobbles; both my skin and tightly bitten nails were safely hidden.

Every Wednesday a new bunch of expensive hybrid flowers arrive at the house, bundled and wrapped by the florists on Davies Street; they are placed in a large vase on the entrance table and the deceased foliage is removed. Today is Thursday, the flowers fresh and ready to burst into full bloom; they are currently a pungent majestic white lily, with some leafy green strands. I loathe them; their scent is so powerful; the pollen visibly floats in the air waiting to be breathed in, resulting in a series of roughly five irrepressible sneezes, and sore, runny eyes. I would happily add them to my list of murders, and so I did. I took a couple of dragon stems upstairs (and I say dragons, for when they're fully open, their ferocious faces look ready to breathe fire on you). There was no sound from any room or landing. I placed one in the completed solution and one in ordinary water. At this point I sat motionless; the effect of the potion would be slow releasing, I remembered this, for the rats had never died immediately but after a prolonged spell, possibly some hours. Eventually I could no longer watch, not out of pain, but out of anticipation, so I left the room quietly, and went to make a pot of tea. This I made so speedily, that I decided on another distraction to pass at least two hours.

I stepped outside onto the pavement and inhaled a deep breath of cloudy air. The freshest I've enjoyed, would be when the grasses are cut on the park lawns in early spring. November holds no such pleasure. I crossed the square to the bench by the railings. It was not yet rush hour, and although we live in the heart of London there are still moments when the song of a late afternoon blackbird can be heard, and the return tune of his fellow neighbour.

I was feeling very drowsy after my intense time in the study. My head was heavy and my limbs moulded into the seat like soft clay. I feared I would be unable to drag myself up, despite the uncomfortable furniture pushing into my flesh; was I being re-formed, restructured? After two hours, for I was a good time-keeper and always looked at my watch, I spoke loudly, *'I must look.'* How I had passed the time is beyond me. I did not doze or fall into exhaustion-induced sleep. I am not in the habit of dozing. It was a great shock to hear myself cry out; I didn't recognise the tone, the accent, the sound of my own voice. I jumped at my own self possessed sharpness. I remind you, so much conversation is held in my head.

I hurried inside, no one had come or gone from the house, and the streets were beginning to swell and become rowdy. Upstairs in the study room I gave a gasp of joy as the lily, which had sat so formally and upright in the potion now lay flat, bruised and ugly on the floor. The other lily inside the bottle of tap water remained unchanged, as arrogant and as proud as before. The method had worked producing a gradual death! I could not measure agony or suffering but while my own personal dignity continued to be scrutinised, the overall effect was of no concern to me. My face stretched with the size of my grin. I wasted no time in gathering the ready solution with its label and two separate lots of two heaped teaspoons of talc, wrapped in dark hankies. This ensured I had sufficient quantities of poison and would not have to return to the poison box. These I placed into my pockets. I tidied the study, returning items to shelves and drawers, cleaning the utensils, until the room looked much the same as before. It was reinstated to its original, dismal, disused status; the remnants of my experiment vanished. I gathered the lilies and the box and carefully disposed of them in a bag, discarding the waste into the local bins. The bins are cleared and cleaned with great punctuality, all before early evening. The evidence was securely erased. I traced my steps back into the house with a watchful eye and guiltless bodily conduct. I felt powerful, I felt invincible.

The next stage of this evolving plan was how to go about it and this, I found, came to mind very easily. Although I see little of my mother and sister there are certain aspects of their lives I have come to know. They have a simple routine. I know my pattern week to week is variable, yet the female members of this household keep regular arrangements. Tonight I would use this knowledge to my advantage.

On Thursdays my sister Sarah invites her friends over for a late evening coffee, which lasts approximately one hour. Some friends are from work and others are old school friends

that have remained in London; her companions change week to week, but there's always an even six in the party. I do not know any of them. On the odd occasion I have stumbled upon one in the hall, should you ask me to distinguish between each one of her gathered group, I'd simply raise my arms and shoulders, exhaling with a shrug *'I can't tell them apart.'*
The voices, the mannerisms, the constant talking and squealing in indecipherable tones, I am not even sure if we speak a common language.

Sarah prepares her coffee set about 7pm for guests at half past eight. This custom of hers I know as well as the hand knows the clock-face. After she has fiddled with cups, saucers, milk jug, sugar and spoons, the tray is left undisturbed and unaltered. When the first guest arrives, Sarah will come down from her bedroom. The water is then boiled, the milk also warmed and a small stash of biscuits arranged on a plate. The countless number of times I have heard the simple, feminine cries of *'no, I mustn't eat a bite!'* or *'you do spoil us!'* Subsequently the plate is returned to the kitchen, scattered in crumbly remains. For some time I have taken a unique interest in the coffee set of six Sarah uses; it is an old family heirloom of the Art Deco style. The body of the cup is straddled in fine silver and black lines with the plain yet elegant design further complemented by a square of unfilled gold. It is a charming collection, however there is one unfortunate fault that mars its complete perfection; one cup carries a small chip on the rim, which would devalue the set, but in my mind enhances it. Firstly this tiny breakage will be my best friend, for it is the cup from which Sarah drinks, she too being aware of its indelicacy will always drink her coffee among friends from the damaged cup. Secondly from an artist's point of view the origin of the chip adds a personal touch; I believe my father would take the cup and use it in his own experimentations before my mother stopped him using it as an indifferent tool and bought him instead a set of cheap science glasses. The chip, and small stain which on closer inspection I spotted, are no doubt the results of his poor vision and careless mixing.

To progress, into this chipped cup I placed half the powdered talc, an estimate of one teaspoon, from the quantity I had wrapped safely away; you will know that a coffee cup is small, holding roughly 150ml. I took this into account on planning a death over a two hour period or more, when the guests were gone (no one ever stayed beyond the first person leaving) and Sarah would be alone in bed.

Every odd, imbalanced and provoking question entering my head was gratifyingly answered; each with an undeniable confidence and self assurance: the exact coffee cup would be used by her and her alone, the taste of the powder would be easily disguised blended into a strong, fragrant coffee, whose heat would instantly permeate the porcelain. I also felt Sarah would be so distracted by her role as hostess; she would not notice or fuss over any subtle difference in flavour or appearance. She had no reason to be suspicious. Good: a clean job done.

My next task involved access to my mother's separate apartment and to quickly assess her night-time provisions before making to bed. I knew she always played cards at a friend's house on Thursday. She and Sarah would agree to catch up with each other on Friday morning; having fatigued their socialising powers late on Thursday. Therefore it's evidential that after 7pm, when my mother left Sarah in the kitchen, they would not see each other again that evening. They would be separated for some time and I could act on them individually without any troubling interference.

The room was much larger than I anticipated; there were articles and clothes scattered all over the place; I was defensive, fearing a stranger may have rummaged through her belongings. What were the chances of being blamed for the act, if I was caught now in this compromising position! It took some minutes before my eyes became accustomed to the dull, early evening grey, deluding my sight like a costume mask. The house was quiet, only the odd rumble of traffic permeated the walls. I fancied walking to the large window, which was fractionally open, to gaze down on all the busy lives below; these are momentary human thoughts, coming in and out of my mind whilst surveying the surroundings. Tonight I was a shadow cast by the light from a small lamp whose low function would not dare illuminate my full presence. However composed the house, I would never let a second pass without thinking about the objective of this personal invasion. Nonetheless each part of the room seemed irresistible; there was a small bookshelf of classical novels, bound in red leather; a selection of British poetry, and some magazines; the walls were decorated in watercolour landscape and still-life paintings of her own hand, and one by Sarah; the bed was covered in vibrantly patterned quilts. Off the bedroom were three smaller rooms, one a cupboard-sized bathroom, in another a tiny kitchen and drinks cupboard, and lastly a walk-in dressing room, which smelt distinctly of peppermint and mothballs. The combination of the two made my stomach heave and my throat tighten, forcing a hand to my mouth. The collection of clothes, shoes, shawls and handbags was vast, and despite finding some strewn on the floor many were hung together as outfits. How mysteriously the mind works at moments like this! My head was active; many thoughts were channelled, recognised and interpreted into a perfect sequence of absolute strength. In writing them all down I take up more space and time than was given to their original formation.

These rooms were easily observed without having to leave the bedroom space. After a few minutes of visual scouring, I found the most attractive piece, for it still lingers in the memory: *'the inward eye is the bliss of solitude'* as Wordsworth once said of daffodils. It was a triple mirrored dressing table, which held all my mother's treasured possessions: perfume, rings, makeup and other jewellery pieces. It was carved in speckled walnut wood, not intricately but certainly lovingly; its simplicity enhanced its beauty. The thin mirror-glass was bevelled and slightly mottled. I did not wish to view my own reflection but I imagined the triple portrait of my mother, as she sat preparing herself for the day, with an array of accessories and tools.

What an occupation for a woman. I never before imagined, the trouble and attention they go to. This perfectionism compares well to the artist and his studio: the brushes, dyes, paints and palettes all prepared for the canvas. My mind was steadfast and decided; heightened by the foresight of my deadly intent. It now became less of a human compulsion and more of a divine providential commitment.

Then one thought did enter my head (maybe it has little relevance or maybe one might read greater things into it). I felt it being printed onto my memory as the tapping of a typewriter. You can never entirely know a person; the face is a facade protecting the truth of inner life. Standing here amongst this stage-set of ingredients it came to me; the emergence or realisation of a character within the actor, what it might feel to be someone else; to experience a whole new set of ideas, values and concerns. These would be things I've never before considered because they had never encroached upon my way of thinking. For example, if I always take the bus, why should I need to understand a train timetable; likewise if I dress in jacket and tie, what does it matter to me what jewellery or scarf to wear with which skirt; or how best to calm a baby. Until we are thrown into these circumstances ourselves we have no need of their frivolous and irrelevant existence.

Scientists look for equations and theories to explain everything; statisticians love numbers and sums and organisation. Artists, however, see the world as an ever creative and unexplained place which cannot be described or reasoned using long theories. I've thought about this many times over and it's best described using the idea of probability. If every day I wake up and have toast for breakfast, the scientist believes I will continue to do so, as statistics have shown, but I am human not robotic; one day I decide to change to cereal (no one can imagine when, because not even I know when it will be) his prediction is wrong. This is the beauty of life under one's own control. What then of averages? How useless are they?! If a room is filled with ten 70 year olds and ten 30 year olds, the average age is 50 years, yet not one of them is 50. To be an average is to say you are ordinary; similar to everyone else. Who would ever want to be that? If a 50 year old walked into the room, they would be unique, not the average.

The focus of my observation was now more determined, as I felt I'd lost some valuable time; a few minutes of thought here and there had slowed my pace. Staring openly at the large bed I needed a quick resolution, lest I should run into unannounced complications. There were two small matching side tables and I tiptoed, taking more caution considering I'd already outstayed the time I had allotted myself, toward the right side: the closest to the main door and my exit. This was clearly her sleeping side, the little table crammed with a still life of objects. These were her most used articles: a novel, a notepad and pencil, a tall Venetian coloured glass, a small non-descript glass with accompanying water, a bottle of wine, corked, close to the end and bordering on the edge of the table, a packet of peppermints, sleeping pills, ointments, a skin cream, a pressed flower and a small cross stitch of a wheelbarrow. What an odd assortment of pieces. In conclusion I made this swift summary: before turning out the small side lamp she sipped a glass of wine, took a sleeping pill and sucked a peppermint for indigestion, closely followed by a little water, then read a page or two of her novel, maybe even scribbled some notes on her pad for the next day; the drowsy effects of the alcohol and pill would soon follow soothingly. Night's dreams awaited, pooling their mix of ideas and imaginings into the mind; if the sleeping pill did not block them, they would be allowed to take root, their consequences retold by day; the voice the echo of the dreamy playwright.

The light was weakening in the room, and the whole task became harder; the wind had picked up and started to disturb some of the shawls and papers. I did not like these solid, seemingly immoveable objects stirred into life; might they gain eyes as well? Once again I felt watched and judged and discomfited; now the internal sounds had begun to take precedent over the outside world. I felt pressed. I could not make a wrong move, distraction had already lost me time, but it would not lose me the opportunity. Minutes ago I'd not been able to count the docile, singular chimes of an overlooked bedside clock. It had awoken nothing within me, except the call of old Father Time; was he warning me or mocking me? Suddenly I realised that if I could not pull myself together, re-gather my mind and pursue my purpose, the firm scrutiny of household patterns would be lost to my own slowness.

I grabbed the wine bottle with unnecessary force, as if it might have come reluctantly; poured out almost all the remaining contents into the small kitchen sink, added some of the readymade solution of poison; then took the plain water, discarded it, and replaced it with the rest of the solution, not a drop was left. I slipped the bottle neatly and resourcefully back into my jacket pocket. The sink had a slight tinge of Spanish red from the wine, which I washed away with minimal fuss and without the use of strong odours. I returned the water decanter and the wine bottle to the side table, nodding at the efficiency and exactness of my moves. It seemed to bring a whole new air of positivity to this moment; I was relieved of the final task.

On leaving the room I allowed my head one last swoop, like an owl surveying its landscape. I caught sight of my reflection in the triple mirror; I was red with perspiration, every nerve in my body felt over-exerted with emotion; if I had run a marathon I would have looked as hot and exhausted. Without meaning to, I stared directly into my eyes and a freezing cold glare of anger, hate and bitterness, came back at me, like the smack of a wet flannel. It seemed to bring me back round; my self control and stamina regaining their strengths. Making confident steps upon the carpet, I took a deep and silent breath, feeding my whole self with a fresh energy; my breathing had resorted to short wheezy panting. Now fully engaged, I bowed to the reflection, turned the door knob and walked out into the hallway.

I can recall so many details of the evening, yet the next few minutes are proving hazy. I know I went directly upstairs to my bedroom. I was exhausted. At some point two vital things must have occurred: one, I discarded the evidence of the poison solution bottle and the poison talc, perhaps back into my father's study, tucked away; two, I had obviously slipped out of my mother's room just in time for there were already girlish voices and greetings coming from the hallway as I ascended the stairs. If I'd been acknowledged or noticed by anyone, it is the back of my unmoving head that would have grazed their vision. My wide eyes and pale-faced complexion felt taught and stung as if shocked by the light bulb inside my own head; an image I imagined to be as haunting as Medusa's glare. I feared possible discovery, for women have infallible powers and instincts; they have understood us before we have understood ourselves.

How and what time I retired to bed, I cannot answer, not even under pain of death would I have been able to describe any of my actions. Tiredness is an effective drug and it clearly hit me more rapidly and desperately than I could have imagined. Thus, I hypothetically state, I fell into bed relieved, slept very deeply, and soundly which is not unusual, but awoke with a shock. There were small beads of sweat all over my forehead and my underarms prickled;

my hair was wet and matted. Nonetheless, unfettered by guilt, I proceeded straight to my desk and took up the nearest pad of paper and pen to record clearly and succinctly the series of events begun the previous evening. The house, my room and the square outside seemed dead and despondent to me, not until I started writing and bringing objects and specific people into focus was the world stimulated, as if I had personally been charged to enliven it.

My story therefore closes. I present it to you now; I give fully and factually for your understanding, the truth, which ultimately will seal my fate.

Aleister Stratton

Part VI

I, Professor Giles, wish to write a footnote here, continuing this story a little further; I can develop the scene where Aleister cannot. I'd listened intently to his descriptive confession for at least an hour, little had disturbed us; the mutter of silence infrequently broken. In one instant several pigeons, observantly noticing our rooted position on the bench, flew down beside us to scavenge for crumbs. Pigeons have always irritated people in London, nesting and brooding in their walls, on buildings and monuments. For me it was refreshing to admire the creature, a symbol of flight and freedom; for once I envied their wings, and their simple life. The dampness had successfully penetrated my bones, I felt chilled all over, far from home, and worst of all stuck in the midst of a ghastly story: hideous and inconceivable. When he ended his monologue, through which I had made no sound nor rendered a question, I realised he had woven me into this tale; might I continue the next chapter? Was I expected to witness the bodies? Dispose of them? Participate in a police inquiry? This morning he'd left for classes knowing full well he was a murderer; he had planned and executed two murders, and the passing of time had allowed the consequences of such actions to augment.

Turning my head to the sky, a dense and agitated mist was extending its oppressive body above our heads; not one star could penetrate this thick layer of gloom; not even a slight, willowy stretch of natural light from the moon. The atmosphere seemed sinister, artificial and compressed, sometimes all at once, cursed by the three witches. I felt alone, empty and bewildered for the first time in a very long time. It reminded me, as Aleister had mentioned in his story, of taking on the sentiments or sensations of someone else. I was unrolling a new part of myself; a part which was undiscovered. In truth I did not like it one bit, far out of my comfort zone and oh how would I deal with it? I even resorted to the clichéd statement of *'this stuff happens to other people but not to me!'* Since the sky was a useless source of succour, I swiftly turned in the direction of Aleister, who, during the telling of his tale, I had not looked at once. His face! How can I begin to describe the pale ghostly profile, the deathly pallor struck by the down light of a lamp post? He truly looked like a disarmed man in battle. With the fear I might disturb the silence we were both soaking up, I chose to follow his stare without interjection. Across the quiet street, one or two cars took a speedy cut-through route, there I caught sight of the source of his disturbance. Two ladies, one much older than the other, the latter perhaps her daughter, sharing the same mannerisms, were illuminated by a rather unflattering lamplight; the light revealing similar features. Aleister's interest in these two women was, at first, not as obvious to me as it may seem to you; they were his two (very much alive) *'murder victims'* chattering away over a door key like sparrows over crumbs. Aleister stood up, which must have caught the eye of the elder lady, the near-silent murky atmosphere provided few people as tall and distinctive as him. Before I could whisper a word to Aleister, the two women were at our bench-side, as if they'd been fired from a canon. I scarcely remember seeing them move, thus proving the point that we're never quite completely absorbed in our present state to wonder about every second laid before us.

Aleister stood motionless. It's extraordinary how, without utterance, the boy was bluntly and rudely reprimanded and embarrassingly scolded by the two whiney women. I sat still like an indifferent weathered statue. I thought of myself as inconsequential and I may pass unrecognised, excluded from this sensitive scene. I do not exaggerate! It soon became quite clear the two ladies were indeed his mother and sister, repeating the other's sentences, and embellishing the endings; highlighting and nodding in agreement to each discussion, every body part in full use. Although my head was lowered I could sense the energy exuding from these women, how lethargic and slow men must seem to them.

Wildly and tiresomely they absorbed all the oxygen from the air, Aleister was surely worn down by the suffocating effect of rants and gesticulations over late buses, slow walkers, tedious queues, kind doctors, and unfriendly staff. Any topic could have been thrown into the air and these ladies would have put all their weight and force behind it. Was this a conversation or a turn to the jury? It sent my ears ringing, my temperature rising and the pang in my stomach, which until now had made the oddest groaning noises, sink reluctantly back down again behind my ribs for merciful protection. While this chastisement continued, I refused to confront the women. My ears had no choice but to listen; my focus fixed at my feet (strangely I had dressed in odd socks, which came as a mild surprise). After some minutes I did turn to look at them, the lamp posts were the only source of consistent light; they provided a good likeness and study. My first thought was they were very much living human beings and Aleister was not the murderer he believed himself to be. This did not absolve him of intent but it certainly eased my mind a great deal. What the discovery did for him I can never be entirely sure, but he was pale, confused and emotionally tortured. May I even write here, *I was genuinely sorry for him.* He looked more worried at seeing them alive, than pronouncing them dead minutes earlier.

However there is a more important point I wish to raise here. Whilst his family babbled away I became aware of his mother's upper lip; it was badly blistered, split and coated in a blotchy redness; it was sore and tender from rubbing, likewise his sister was suffering from a sore throat, causing her mouth to dry up and speech to be strained and raspy. Then I realised the course of their unbelievably extended set of moans had, in summary, been a visit to the late night chemist to enquire over their afore-mentioned ailments and the best medicine to relieve the symptoms. They'd both woken with equal pain that morning. Comparing each other's discomfort and the oddity of them both suffering such disfigurements, they'd decided to visit their favourite and trusted local doctor who works in the evening.

I was not sure if Aleister was well enough to take any of this in. I believe, from observing a sudden sharp glint to his eyes, washing colour into his gleaming pupils, he *had* noticed what I had noticed. He stood in a trance as if frozen externally in time but warmed internally by another power.

Without introduction, or interest, the two women (having found their door keys) scurried back across the road like dormice to their door. They opened the front door giving them access to their world inside the large house I had spent over an hour staring at blankly.

Aleister did not turn back to me. He'd already handed me the sheets of paper, those you have read previously. All he could muster, in an ordinary and mundane tone was,

"Something has been done, but not as I thought."

Desperately keen to make my own way home, I set off. My blood, having rapidly chilled, began gradually to re-heat and to filter through my system; I felt mildly agreeable and natural again. Picking up a good pace, I started to repeat Aleister's parting phrase over and over again; thrusting it into my memory, willing it to make sense. I failed. Perhaps warming up would do the trick, but the line still fell cold. I tried it in a range of voices, like experimenting with different type fonts until you find the most fitting for your work. With a hint of menace it produced (and I found this out quickly enough), an ominous delivery: dry and cutting. I could not blame an absent wind for the intermittent shivers down my back; my shoulders hunched like a loose prisoner and my gait the slant of a drunkard.

The turbid sky, which earlier had shown little sign of empathy with the meddling mist, gave grace to a nearly-perfect moon. *'What a relief.'* I remember thinking. Its' reflection turned the muddiness of dull puddles into small, dotted moonstone mines; they glistened magically. Odd figures darted through the avenues casting gymnastic shadows on the tall buildings, their bodies as distorted as their silhouettes. It appeared that all the Mannerist men of the night trundled their obscure, extended shapes under cover of darkness - only the moon could make out these irregular forms. In this short time I, too, became one of these nocturnal victims: dragging their limbs and ashamedly hiding their adult fears.

Part VII

I awoke with a jerk, mid-morning on the Saturday, leaning over the side of the bed as if teetering on the edge of a precipice. Beside me, on the rug, and in innocent comfort, snored Lolly, our Springer spaniel; her floppy, shaggy ears drooped over her eyes. I watched her wet nose twitch in time to the sound of her snores. The smell of well-cooked toast wafted upstairs into the bedroom and I lay on my back, breathing in the smoky, crusty air of homely temptations. Despite the cosiness of my situation, snuggled deep in the folds of a feathery duvet, with two oversized pillows for support, the rest of my body started to tingle and my mouth watered as the sense thickened. Charred on the edges but worthy of a good scrape of butter and jam or maybe marmalade, complemented with a strong tea and two sugars. The drifting fragrance fed the imagination. Toast, a wonderful invention, no doubt come across by mistake - perhaps if I got some of the right things wrong occasionally, new and even better things might be born? I was confused; parts of my head mixed up like a jigsaw, the pieces were all there, just not fitting together correctly. My stomach grumbled (*'when had I last eaten?'*) and my muscles overcame their exhaustion, re-energised themselves, eager to indulge my cravings as urgently as possible.

After hastily washing and dressing, the kitchen table was a perfect sight. *'Thank you my dear wife!'* However, prior to the first tantalising bite, we began the conversation every couple sits down to in the morning, with additional questions.

"How did you sleep, you were home late, is everything ok?" My wife asked firmly, but endearingly. Am I supposed to answer all at once or comment on each individually? If I just said *'yes'* would that suffice? I pondered, blew the steam from the teacup, wishing I could do the same to my overloaded brain, just blow the invisible vapours away with a couple of puffs. The realities of last night began to resurface. I could have no better ally than my wife, yet this was something I needed to mull over, before I could divulge all I'd learnt.

"I slept very well, very deeply, despite Lolly." I said, taking a large, crunchy bite and eyeing the hungry look Lolly held, obediently waiting for a crust to flip off my plate and upturn its buttery side onto the floor.

"There's a student at school whose struggling with his coursework, we talked about it all last night, I think he's just going through a tough time,

not making friends, some family issues, nothing abnormal." This was as straightforward as I could have presented it, except maybe the last part about *'being abnormal.'* Aleister was the most peculiar boy I had ever come across, the very epitome of abnormal. I needed time to reorganise my thoughts.

My wife sighed sympathetically, *"Well I hope you can help him, it's a vulnerable, complicated age. Have a word with Tessa; she rang yesterday evening to catch up; she loves the seaside life."*

Of course, my sister Tessa, Dr Nottingham, who had been at the forefront of my thoughts yesterday. She'd moved to the coast 2 years ago, finally retiring from her clinical practice to establish herself outside the city, working from home on a part time basis. It was proving a true success.

"Yes I'll call her, thanks, it's time we got together." I replied.

"Just leave me a note if you're going out," called my wife from the hallway as she jangled Lolly's lead. Poor Lolly she had missed out on her crust, desperate to anticipate the accidental drop to the floor; we did this every morning. I would act so ridiculously surprised, she would wag her tail eagerly, I'm amazed it's still attached to her; my wife would rub the

dog's soft snout affectionately. She would then kit herself out for a long, muddy, wet walk and Lolly would prance out of the kitchen like the prize champion. However there had been a significant shift in my life since the previous night; this was not of my doing or wanting but it had specifically come to find me out. Now I understood what it was to be a dog on the scent; there were unanswered questions and problems to solve, consequences to come and I could not leave them alone. Already I was feeling the effect of a chain reaction of events. I was keen to resolve matters over the course of the weekend and had one hopeful idea in my head: Tessa.

After several attempts on the phone, and receiving an engaged tone, not once but twice thereby deliberately making a simple call, difficult, I finally spoke to Tessa. She was pleased to hear from me, and not at all disconcerted by my sudden keenness to invite myself down for a long day by the coast. Although she did have some clients in the morning, her afternoon was entirely free, and I jokingly booked myself in for a session with her. I was worried when she took this quite seriously but Tessa was always the consummate professional. When I explained I had a student I wished to discuss with her I was still not sure she believed me, and then I felt like the younger brother again. Was I somehow forming sympathies with Aleister and his situation? No, not at all, any similarities that occurred were purely coincidental; I would not let an ounce of his mentality rub off onto me. Somehow I couldn't quite slip out of the little brother role; it's not necessarily something that's said, it's the way it's said, and those tiny irritations that siblings have between one another can be rekindled very quickly, even when they're not face to face. This was one of those moments. Besides, I needed her, so would have to tolerate the sisterly issues, and I knew she would thrive on the information I would bring her. We could both consider it a fair and pleasing prospect. We made brief arrangements. I scribbled a speedy but legible note to my wife, telling her not to worry about *this* evening. My whereabouts were totally in the hands of Tessa's tolerance and the efficiency of the railway system.

It was easier to walk the distance to the station than risk getting stuck in congestion as the taxi meter clicked up a hearty sum, costing more than a lunch out for two. I was glad to leave London, to shake up my senses, move the limbs, and even air my coat from last night's meeting. It was a strange walk to the train terminus, everyone I casually perused, looked familiar; I felt I had seen most of them somewhere before. Their faces were recognisable but not place-able; I tried to make eye contact hoping the recipient might shed light on the way my mind was working. I tried very hard to find a position for them. Perhaps from a TV programme, a student's associate, maybe a student, another teacher, someone from the papers, a shop I frequented, a market I went to. Impossible, it was one of those curious sets of circumstances, as if life had been pre-determined. I directed one person to Oxford Street, but they were foreign, they lip-read my response with such deep concentration and intense examination over my gestures, I even believed I'd previously met them too. This refreshing, if somewhat confusing walk, helped to re-set my brain. At last the weather delivered a sunny, sapphire-blue sky. We had been suffering 23 consecutive days of intense and interminable gloom. The grey clouds descending over our heads like leaden balloons. Occasionally they shifted a great body of heavy, inconvenient rain, lashing at straining umbrellas with irrepressible anger. Day after indistinguishable day, unrelenting and persistent, it continued to nag and frustrate my mild temper. It wasn't so much the rain; it was the short, closed-in day; the threatening invasion of moody, usurping clouds, stealing the sun. I missed colour. The palette of winter is dismally bleak.

Today brought a sun to warm my cheeks, everything looked brighter and more cheerful; the light shone all around and even little flecks of milky, spitting rain seemed attractive and defined. Even the ugly parts of London and the ingrained dirt of the city seemed to glow, mirrored against a bright blue sky and more appreciative to the eye. If the backdrop and lighting are flattering then the object lends a more pleasing appeal.

The central station was not as busy as a weekday, and although it had never crossed my mind as to the crowding potential of the train, I still found myself remarking on the quietness. I purchased a return ticket from a very fed up man who was clearly bored to tears with his job; the friendlier I was, the grumpier he became and since this was going to be yet another long and difficult day for me I was happy just to let him be; I half expected him to growl behind the counter, instead he yawned right in my face. I moved swiftly off to the barriers, checked the departure board: final destination, Hastings. I boarded the train like a child off on a country adventure. Trains draw into the city with reluctance and fatigue, but there's something exhilarating about departing trains from London as they glide out of the platform, escaping their confinement and imparting a great sense of anticipation and promise.

Those people I saw arrive from the country seemed fresh-faced; those departing were white and strained. *'How did I appear?'* I wondered. Well my wife would have said *'normal'* and so would Tessa. I was plain, ordinary and normal. I could blend into any environment, not to say adapt, that suggests a whole other meaning, but I would certainly not come across as *'awkwardly out of place.'*

I chose a quiet carriage with a large table, bypassing families munching on wrapped up rolls, Cornish pasties and singing sea shanties; this would have tipped the balance of my tolerance level. I spread myself out comfortably; I had my indispensible bag of essentials (I would not let the confessional papers Aleister had handed me leave my sight). It was also a valuable item for safe-guarding my privacy and for possessing the seat beside me. I was preoccupied and had no idea how this meeting would go or what its outcome would be. I made a brief summary of the compartment.

There was one man absorbed in his book, and two ladies who were nattering at the level of a low-frequency radio channel; I couldn't make out their conversation, it simply merged into a pleasant and acceptable hubbub. They each provided a sense of normality and reality to the trip. I rested, well established in the snug corner of my seat, with lifted feet, catching the intermittent wafts of warm air, rising from the dusty heating system. The train pulled out of the station, and my first clear sight heralded the magnificent River Thames, The Embankment and The Houses of Parliament. I suddenly felt a surge of great pride, as if I might have been responsible for the sky line of this majestic city and its glorious embodiment of power and prestige. My head nodded with authority and acquiescence at the stability this view represented.

As the journey fulfilled its first hour, the stops became more frequent; the air, as the automatic doors opened and closed, was moist and clean. Despite it being November, the fields were rich, earthy, and deeply churned; the woodland clumps were brown and sparse, except for the tiny winter blossoms, sprouting from the tree ends like twinkling nightlights. This is an odd description, but a worthy one; when the wind blew through their tiny, almost naked branches, the raw white and pinkish petals shimmered. My distracted eyes flickered over the window, the rhythmic motion of the train was soporific and easing my over-worked mind, I dozed off.

After a light sleep, the journey seemed to throw me into many different moods. I was reminded of the first verse of *'Spellbound'* a poem by *Emily Bronte* I had read only last week:

> *'The night is darkening round me*
>
> *The wild winds coldly blow;*
>
> *But a tyrant spell has bound me*
>
> *And I cannot, cannot go.'*

Why I should remember it now, on a train, I have no idea. Perhaps I was really unwinding. Some thoughts dominate and command instant attention, blocking those peripheral, more personality enhancing areas. Giving our head space and time allows us to re-order and resuscitate ideas suppressed by daily pressures. It is these that give us our individuality and distinguish us from others.

At last the coast came into view, a thick, dark grey pencil-line on the horizon and whips of chalk-white on the surface. Yes, the sea, distant, but alive and real. The conductor announced the station and within a few minutes the doors slid aside. The young sea shanty–singing family (galloping up stairs, two at a time), several youngsters, some city types and elderly sorts, in fact an entire cross-section of people, as well as myself, stepped-off and disassembled ourselves onto the platform.

I now had approximately 2 hours to myself. I joined the throng of people now leaving the station, those from the train and their friends and relatives who had come to pick them up. I had a rough idea of the direction and layout of the town from my visit of a year ago. I'd considered returning in a spring or summer month, but honestly, I make no excuses; the time had simply disappeared. I took the long route into town; through the new-build section, under the underpass and directly out onto the promenade: a good, flat, straight walk. The salty winds were behind me. I glanced fleetingly over my shoulder at the pier, which stood solid and dependable despite a century of weather and the sea waves licking at its steel legs. The beach was deserted; it was not safe for swimmers or sailors. Seagulls sat on abandoned picnic tables; they were wise not to be flying, the upper air current would tear their wings; the sky here was filled with thin clouds, as if their attractive doughy plumpness had been stretched and rolled like pastry. The sun caught a fishing boat returning from a morning of harvesting the sea; few seagulls trailed it. Small flags on its stern were flying frenetically and it dipped and bowed. It concerned me and made me feel queasy; I gained an un-seaworthy stomach. The contemplation of their excursion and the absorption of this feeling was the last thing I needed. I was already carrying around the thoughts of Aleister Stratton; I didn't need a fishing stomach as well.

I followed the main cobbled street, neatly hidden behind small terraced sea-front homes. Its eclectic mix of cafes and shops were a perfect distraction for me. I enjoyed the out of date shop windows with their aged books, worn furniture and the eccentric clothing and seaside oddities; a rubber duck dressed as a pirate or a wooden seagull doorstop or a smuggler's box of biscuits. What I had remembered most from my last visit to Hastings were the little alleys and passageways that stemmed from the key roads; they often led to peoples' homes but there was always public access to view more of the secrets of the town. They were known locally as twitterns and devised to ease the escape of smugglers fleeing the customs officers. I found them intriguing, and promptly exhausted myself by climbing up and down any little openings I could find. My voyage of discovery through small squares filled with pot plants and antiquated fishing accessories: old lobster pots, a disused buoy, a rusting anchor or some rotting shafts of drift wood. November is not the best month to summarise any British seaside town and it would be unfair to form firm opinions of it, but I was rather relishing my freedom, exploring new aspects of life and living!

I moved on to the museums, further down on the wide, pebbly beach. The Shipwreck museum was a fascinating place with its stories, artefacts and analysis of the old Company ships and their trade routes. The Fisherman's museum, with its life size boat in the centre and its walls adorned with life at sea, brought about the sea sickness again. What a land-lubber I was amidst such bravery! The camaraderie of these men, their strength, the inevitable dangers and the unenviable tasks they faced each day was admirable (a fitting nautical term!). There were small groups of people beginning to enter the museum; I added a contribution to the money box and headed back out into the blustery wind. All this activity and saltiness had worked up an appetite. Strangely enough I didn't fancy fish: battered, smoked or pan fried, not even cockles, whelks, unshelled prawns or a pint of jellied eels. I'd made a mental note on arrival of a simple cafe in the first cobbled street, but there was no view of the sea. I noticed most of the sea-front cafes had begun to fill with up with coach-loads of travellers and day-trippers. I didn't want to get caught in the wrong crowd and find myself trapped in a coastal party with a special set lunch. Checking my watch I still had a good 45 minutes, and since I'd already broken the boundaries of my normal Saturday pursuits I thought *why not go a bit further still, try something else.'* The whiff of hot oil and the shaking of pans from The Blue Mermaid Chip Shop were an irresistible temptation for a Londoner. No queue, I went straight in. I know it's not healthy or wise, but this had gradually become a little holiday and that was all the justification needed. I ordered a large bag of hot chips to take away; the young man at the counter smiled at the expression on my face. I must have appeared like an old school boy, checking myself should I be reprimanded at any moment. I covered them in salt, a little vinegar, bought a milky tea in a polystyrene cup and headed south to sit on the beach.

There was a sheltered spot overlooking the lifeboat base and the harbour arm. There was a little working activity; one fishing boat was being hauled in by a tractor, not the one I'd seen earlier, this was much larger, with different colourings and flags. On the shoreline they were wrapping and mending the nets; their shouts were inaudible, the fishermen no doubt had their own language. It was here I sensed the traditional oak-smoking custom; it tinged the corners of my nose and altered my taste buds. The pungent particles used the airborne currents to enlighten my sensibilities. I trembled like a guilty smuggler and held the precious hot-wrapped chips close to my chest. About five seagulls sat nearby on barnacled posts. The gulls winked at me encouragingly, shuffling themselves a little closer when I turned my head. Their long, sharp beaks were light-yellow in colour, with a tint of ketchup red on the hook. I didn't share a scrap.

Part VIII

I knocked on the door of cottage number 6. There was no answer, and for a second, (momentarily effective enough to cause mild confusion) I thought I'd disturbed the wrong number. Tessa took some time to answer; I pondered the other cottages, all tastefully decorated (there were only six in total and hers had a double aspect at the top end). In the window of number 5, an older woman with curly hair and flower-printed blouse stared out at me, I mouthed '*hello*' and she withdrew. Aside from her, I assumed the little line of cottages were empty. From this elevated position you could hear the shouts and screams of children on the fairground below, the calls from dog walkers and the respondent yelps, up on the cliff behind. There were many distant, scene-filling sounds, only here was it inactive; I suppose you might call it '*tranquil*'. Too remote for a Londoner, but then maybe that's exactly why they did come down here: to escape. Perhaps the cottages were full of peaceful, serene spaces, just as the occupiers intended. I walked up a few steps to where the individual gardens lay; they were not attached to the cottages, but laid out neatly in rows. There were four narrow slithers of land each looking weather worn and winter beaten. In summer they'd make lovely patches of green, filled with an array of flowers and herb tubs. Now there were only the odd Latin labels, their photos of richly dressed and abundant plants, stuck to the slimy ceramic. If you sat at a small round table, the seasonal view of the distant shimmering sea would be dazzling; forever changing the colours of its spectacular body. I imagined warm sunsets of lambent light in whose mood one reflected a subdued gentleness of absolute serenity, swept away by the pink glow of the sunbeams and their outstretched arms. With a wider perspective you could see the ferry boats and cruise liners, the white sails and the curling offshore breakers. This was a private oasis. I heard the key turning in the door; Tessa said farewell to a young lady, who shyly left the cottage; she bid her take care on the slippery paving stones. I made my approach from behind the bushes. We said our hellos. I was happy to see her and she mirrored an informal delight.

Tessa made a pot of tea and I settled into her warm cottage, cosying up to the fire like a dog on a shaggy rug. We talked for some time about the weather, life in London and on the coast, the town and my mini exploration around it. She had retired from psychology and therapy in

London; work she loved. In the last 4 months she'd decided to take up some clients again. There was a photo of Clive, her husband, on the mantelpiece; he had died five years ago. I think she couldn't cope with his loss in the London house; she never said much about it, she didn't need to, it was understandable and although we had never been hugely close, in terms of talking, I'd felt her grief as much as any sibling. I'm not sure her own therapy could help her however comprehensive her studies of the mind. The presence of a universal spirit and the genetic connection between us had related all it needed; she was miserable and mourning inconsolably. I could not weep with her or hug her, but what I had done was frame a photograph of Clive, as he was when we'd all first met him. She'd gazed at it thoughtfully; I watched the emotion run instantly through her body, like sugar in the blood, and then lastly it appeared softly on her face; a smile I had not seen in years. I think it renewed some of her faith again, this and moving away.

Once I started on the tea, a fine porcelain cup of it, I began very comfortably with my story. It was fresh in mind and I was certain not to miss out any vital details.

I need not reiterate the tale here, for you have read it yourselves, all too well do you know my predicament. Tessa had the gentlest eyes, everything I said was absorbed by them; I thought of her as a thirsty plant taking up water, it took pleasure in growing into something stronger and wiser.

I did not dramatise the event; beginning with Aleister's entrance into my study, to our floundering escapade through London, to his candid revelation on the bench, and his certain shock on seeing his relations alive. I retraced each step slowly through my mind, reliving every moment. After an hour, when I was tired of my own voice and drained by salty breezes; my energies could not be replenished by food or drink, only a good night's sleep. The walk earlier had weakened me; I was not disappointed in myself for having exerted such enthusiasms but there was no more I could say. If I'd been delivered of more determination, or more pep, the words would still not come. Tessa had, intentionally, encouraged me to talk. Frequently I watched questions enter her head, by the time she had sighed or *'ummed,'* they'd been answered fully enough; a nod or fluttery blink seemed to confirm this too. I handed her Aleister's handwritten story in which he explains his methods and guilt, and my personal footnote. There was no feeling of bias on my account; she took both in earnest.

Then, quite simply, it was over. I'd shared the responsibility faithfully; I believe it to be in much better hands. Dwelling on my situation in wonderment, I questioned: *'what was I expecting to come out of this?'* I couldn't answer my own mind. I suppose the last line Aleister had uttered to me before he grudgingly retreated (by grudgingly I do not mean a sorry boy who has lost a card game, I mean a pitiful and defeated curve of the body indicating submission).

"Something has been done, but not as I thought."

Perhaps he *did* know more than I realised; it had prompted me to take this whole matter more seriously. In the capable mind and hands of Tessa I felt less ill at ease, as if I had been liberated from a portion of financial debt, yet I could still sense an imbalance, disproportionate to my revelations; a heavy weight flattened my feelings.

Tessa paid the utmost attention and granted my story the solemnity it deserved. She promised to post her analysis within a week and thus using her depth of knowledge and past experience, she was confident she had all she needed to reach a conclusion. I knew the following week's wait would be a struggle. She was meticulous, allowing no written commitment to pass through her hands until she'd thoroughly approved its content.

I thanked her profusely; she curved her lips into a quaint smile and squeezed my hand tightly, saying in a low voice,
"It is I who should thank you." The hushed words delivered full of kindness and sisterly warmth, without a hint of condescension. I stood blankly for a few minutes, yet long enough to picture a mellow pink peep from under her cheeks, rise and then vanish into the pigment's poor, pale cousin.
It's difficult to convey the tones of a voice when writing; an ordinary remark is easily twisted by the reader. Sometimes without realising it, they've altered the mildness or intensity of the word and the story is introduced and shifted into a new thought process.

Despite my tired mind, my body was agitated. I decided to walk, taking the opportunity to satisfy the late afternoon.
The wild wind of the morning had exhausted its anxieties onto Earth leaving the land befuddled

and untidy; some of the trees swept up by the strength of the sea winds had a permanent bend, crippled by their forceful persistence: an old wound in their backs. The branches looked strained and contorted, gripping to the trunk like a witch's broom. With those testing winds gone, the time spent outdoors would be a passable one. The colour began to drain out of the sky and seep into the sea, turning it a darker, impenetrable grey-green. I'd learnt this sky-sensing technique at scouts' training many years ago, and this, plus a personal sensation, had always proved invaluable. I'd rescued many boys stranded in torrential storms, whilst tent building in the middle of a field, because they refused to heed my intuition and reading of the sky.

The Old Town was located in a deep valley, bordered either side by two cliffs: East and West. The West side was a green open field accessible by a sharp rise of steps or by meandering along tightly rising roads. A strip of path in the centre curved over the cliff's belly and down into the modern district. The East side was a great, protected sight of ancient broom and hedgerows, wild gorse and ferns, but also a wide plain from which to view more of the coastline, weathered coves and undulating pastures; a mix of rough, fallow farm fields and woodlands. I can describe the East view in detail because I spotted a small Victorian lift cut into the cliff face: the funicular, a typical engineering feat of Victorian genius, a mechanical device created in order to reach the higher areas of ground for exercise and recreation. For £2 I took the 3 minute ride to the top, the penultimate trip before close of day. This avoided the challenge of a few hundred adjacent steps of differing treads. As my compartment went upwards so another compartment came down, balancing the run with precision; peering over to the downside carriage I recognised the family from the train. The mother and father of two looked frayed and depleted, while the children appeared to be squabbling and scrambling about. One child waved to me and I waved back, surprised at my own involuntary action. Previously it would have pleased me to think they were headed in the opposite direction and preparing to take an earlier train home. However, two new thoughts entered my head before I had a chance to happily gloat on this certainty; firstly, what a joy it was to see such animated children, whose little lives had been so stimulated by their unforgettable experiences in Hastings; secondly, *'what makes one child turn so fatally aggressive towards his relations, as Aleister had done?'*

At the top was a small turreted building, modelled on castle defence structure; up here I was one of few. The air was even fresher and the view, clearer, invigorating and more breathtaking than ever. Looking beyond the town and far out to sea, I garnered a whole new perspective. The ground was muddy with white sullied chalk deposits and stubborn flint stones; they all stuck keenly to my boots. I shook off some of the tightness and relaxed my jaw muscles. The view offered 360 degrees of purity; I had stepped into a landscape painting of one third land and two thirds sky. Often one feels very small in big places, particularly in London, yet here I felt the smallness of humanity unite with the bounty of nature, welcoming each other, embracing me into this picture of harmony. My soul felt replenished and cleansed. I visually traced the majority of the movements I'd made that day; the museums, the cobbled streets, the chip shop; the twitterns hidden from the naked eye, making them a perfect route for smugglers, escaping the dangerous pursuit of the armed Victorian customs men.

I returned to sea-level via the steps; a slanted street wound its way to the bus shelter and a large open space, made of reclaimed and washed local shingle. There were two small huts on this space; I had made out their delicate frames from the cliff edge. I was inquisitive to realize their function and discover what secrets they held, if any. So far this town had delivered all sorts of curiosities; I knew these structures would not disappoint. The first hut, lying close by a park of children's fairground rides, most of which were now closed and covered in blue tarpaulin, was a weather hut. It dated back to 1875 and was about the size of a Punch and Judy stand. It presented and charted the daily weather report on a board, having been recorded and collected twice daily from the West cliff monitoring system. The statistics laid out for the previous month made fascinating reading; even for one who feared numbers, units, degrees and measurements. From the rainfall to cloud cover, from hours of sun to wind direction, every day broken down and detailed to form the final summary. It was the dedicated job of a volunteer, ably filled through the generations; providing copious amounts of information from which you gain ten minutes joy, but remember very little.

The second little hut, sitting opposite the weather hut but more centrally placed within the square, was a camera obscura. I entered through a black curtain which swung back into place as I walked through. In the middle was a stark white circular table that spun round as I touched it and above it two pulley ropes with rough, peeling labels reading *'pull slowly'*. I obeyed this random scribble and then followed the instructions, making the assumption that if encouraged to do so, something remarkable would happen. Carefully pulling the ropes turned the camera sitting on the roof; this in turn formed a picture on the table of the immediate outside, adjusting it I could form a sharp image. The picture displayed the fishing boats, slightly misshapen and berthed awkwardly on the working beach, the net shops and the mini railway line. Unbeknown to them the camera eye allowed me a unique advantage; I could witness the wind-swept passerby and bounding dog, all captured to view. It was starting to feel intrusive. I'd spent an afternoon releasing my fears, seeking a clarity and explanation, but life had again become tightly focused within this small frame. Suddenly I felt claustrophobic, hidden inside this little hut, the world closing in around me.

I left and made for the station, the simplest and quickest route I could remember. Once I'd decided to return home, the longing made me walk faster and without turning back. I could sense a storm brewing in the sky, ready to engulf me, flaking off pieces of cloud to unsettle me. The light lingered, faintly attached to the sky before the Earth pasted a dark, velvety covering over its muted complexion and the stars emerged like tight pins to keep it in place. I'd stayed out too long and was eager to take the next city train and return to the illuminated skies of London.

The journey went like a flash. Whether my mind was sleeping or I actually slept and shut it down willingly, I have no exact recollection. From the platform gates I headed directly to the taxi stand where I waited over 45 minutes with a group all champing at the bit to start their Saturday night in the capital. My exertions of the day were over and without interference or conversation I was silently whisked along the backstreets, smiling with familiarity at every turn. It was nigh on 8pm by the time I fumbled with keys and entered the house. My dear wife greeted me with a hug and a tender kiss. For the last part of the trip I'd sensed an oppressive chill; a sluggish lethargy had reached my core. Now home, I was ready to be warmed and nourished again, and saved sensually by the intoxicating smell of baking apple crumble; sweet bubbling apples coated in a mix of fragrant spices, finished with a classic buttery, crunchy topping. There was custard too, what bliss! My temperature began to rise again and with the remedy of a hot drink pulsing round my body, the numbness subsided and life reawakened. Lolly, and her wagging tail, hurtled toward me with a chewed slipper. *'How could I be angry?'* I wasn't, I couldn't have been happier; she grinned directly at me. There was even a bit of crumble caught in her shaggy ears; she tilted her head, faking an innocent surprise as I brushed it out. After today I think I loved her and my world of habitual lassitude even more.

Part IX

Monday morning arrived with its calendar regularity, groaning with obedience; an aura of trepidation running over it. Lessons were scheduled as usual; structure and routine presided throughout the day: two classes in the morning, a mid morning break of 15 minutes, four more classes, an hour for lunch; maybe a book club session or extra tuition and marking, then three shorter classes or study periods before the final bell. This sequence and precision helped to calm my spirits after a bizarre weekend. Aleister was present and ordinary, just as he'd been at the end of last Friday. My study, the classrooms and entrance hall stood as places of stability and knowledge, of wisdom and guidance. Not one boy would dare make a mockery in this place of high learning.

I watched him tentatively all week, without overly directing my attention towards his behaviour, which remained passive: no cries, no disputes. His essays were neat, punctual and well researched; he continued to impart a functional attitude to his work. He blended into the background picture of studious boys and classroom system.

It was me who seemed restless; my whole body felt vulnerable to sudden sounds and the call of my name filled me with apprehension. I waited each day for the arrival of Tessa's analysis of Aleister and his story.

I thought the letter would never come. Maybe I'd upset Tessa, without meaning to, and she would not reply. A singular feeling of dread overcame me; I was choking on my own tension, the strain was building; my foods tasted too salty or too sweet, I left much of my breakfast, skipped lunch and ate forkfuls at supper. This magnified my mind's anxieties. By the fourth day I was as fractious and petulant as an over-tired child; I had completely lost faith and resilience. It was not until Friday's late post I received a large brown envelope from the South Coast. Even then it took me some time to open it, pacing back and forth, as if it were the expected results of an exam paper. My wife and Lolly were out on the Heath on Saturday morning, a week having passed since my seaside outing. I felt ready to read Tessa's analysis, whether it proved concise and helpful, long and disagreeable or a complicated series of generalisations. I enclose the documents sent to me.

Analysis of Aleister Stratton by Dr Tessa Nottingham based on the sources presented to me: Aleister's own hand and the hand and mouth of his trusted and honest Professor Giles.

On many occasions it is not easy or practical to meet with a client, in fact sometimes direct contact is ill advised; distance allows perspective; a clear, unaffected and uncluttered mind can be extremely beneficial. As a doctor I prefer using first hand information to logically build a picture much greater than the one displayed on meeting the client. We can take out the disruption, interference and distraction, if a detailed portrayal of the person is set before us. And so I find myself in this very position.

It's sometimes clearer to visualise people by using the colloquial theory of *'coat-hanging.'* By this I mean we can gather and collect clients, placing them under the same branch or umbrella. Nonetheless, there are still huge variations and levels of personality stored within them. Aleister Stratton is afflicted with a personality disorder; it does not appear in the day, it surfaces at night and only in his dreams. A psychopath is characterised by his tendency to commit violent acts and a failure to feel any guilt or regret. His mind is unstable and he upholds no sense of moral responsibility; in truth he has an imperfect control of his mind. Essentially Aleister embodies these elements entirely but only on the fringe of his subconscious. This area of the mind is highly complex and difficult to access and if we are unable to control our own outbursts or irregularities then why should we be able to account, prescribe and evaluate others? We do not tell our lungs to breathe or our heart to pump every second, so why should we be able to control every thinking aspect of our minds safely? The conscious makes us aware of our thoughts and motivations; we can determine our choice of action to a certain extent, as where to go or what to eat.

What if the subconscious abuses its relaxed night time status to activate a horrific idea, as fearsome and gruesome as murder? Imagine one morning you wake up and believe you have committed a murder. It is the indescribable complexity and depth of mind that has acted out the most devious undertaking, yet on waking one discovers nothing has changed. This is exactly the result for Aleister. The scenes he experienced through the subconscious creation were so vivid and intense, the procedure and narrative so precise to him, they are in fact a reality. To us, no such murder has taken place and he is cleared immediately of a crime; for a murder in the mindset is, of course, not a convictable offence. The deaths are falsities and no guilty verdict can prevail. One might say, in sufferance for the boy, it is, and I use the term lightly, a death of his own recalcitrant imagination. You rightly state, one cannot un-know something. It is also true no-one can re-enter the innocence of childhood or cling to youth and boyish flair.

Some people might treat this as 'a bad dream or a nightmare' but it's not always fair to simplify or define it thus. I have heard of mild cases on the subject of *'the creativity of the subconscious.'* Using an example to reference this point; there was once a man who 'dreamt' he had received a prestigious job promotion. He had taken the interview, met the new boss and enjoyed the privileges of his new post. On returning to work the next day, he discovered to his horror, it had been a figment of his imagination and his elevation had not taken place at all. Sometimes many dreams and nightmares are too faint, or unimportant, or a jumble of incomprehensible ideas which, during the day, do not materialise into sense or cohesion. Often they're stronger and persist a little longer into the day before being pushed into irrelevance.

The question is, how safe are we from the complexities of our mind? What we do by day is one thing, how we pass the night is another. In some way we are all capable of being murderers and sentencing our souls; we never know where our subconscious may take us. Its powerful possibilities are frightening; it may lead to highly developed, destructive outcomes or be diluted into a suppressed but receptive vacuum. Physical bullying is visual: the marks are obvious to the eye but Aleister talks of *'belittling,'* of unkind *'insinuations'* and *'insults.'* All are forms of mental bullying and can themselves bring about a myriad of problems, increasing over a long period. In this case his repressive childhood paranoia will, without certainty or warning, bring about catastrophic results.

If a colony of ants, build their home under the structure of your house, scratching out the soil, it will eventually cause the outline to become fractured, weak and vulnerable. What about a manifestation of mice? Manifestation is a repulsive word with unforeseen and unpredictable consequences. Therefore if we bring to the mental sense a manifestation of conflict whereby the subconscious overwhelms the conscious, we can begin to understand how hard living normally can be. If you sow a dark seed, water it with critical words, you grow an angry adult. Perhaps for life's sake *'the sleeping palace of the legend'* is the safest place to hoard dark thoughts, better than to activate them into real truths. Aleister may diligently and quietly continue with his coursework, but his conscious exertions find it desperately hard to maintain his subconscious strengths; his body flanked in a cape of gloomy darkness.

Aleister is a bright child, perhaps a fallen angel in rebellion, whose young soul is solitary and brooding; a damned original, tormented by unusual powers and unlikely to ever find a peaceful or harmonious equilibrium.

I think the most fascinating, yet appalling part of his story comes at the end, which is why we should not dismiss his troubles as bad dreams or nightmares. We must assume Aleister, and you, caught sight of his relatives' blisters, sores and red lips. These abnormalities caused them great angst and upset, over which they made an understandable fuss. Aleister's last remark to you, or even to himself, the one that plagued you and has persuaded you to further your enquiries, sheds light on the workings of his brain and the awareness of his own power, *'something has been done, but not as I thought.'*

I must return to the subject of manifestation. For Aleister, it is the combination of his tormenting female relations and the interpretation of his late father's words: *'take an element of your life and to it blend your imagination.'* Aleister has conjured his dream so forcefully, with such intense passion, that the subconscious ideal has manifested itself into a reality; not by being a whole truth, for his victims are at least alive, but the methods of the murder are visually represented by the scarring sores. It did not achieve the result he intended but it did herald a warning of what his brain could be capable of producing. For Aleister the punishment will be of his making.

I cannot say for certain how Aleister will use his mind in the future but I would say, at such an influential age, it may progress into a deeper and stronger, more affecting dominance. He will most likely remain a nonchalant, detached young man of insouciance; he'll no doubt become an excellent actor, once he has practised the extent of his creative abilities.

Can he be helped? As I said before, the mind is a delicate and dangerous tool. I can't comment on whether it is a recoverable condition, only that it needs to be checked by kind and careful eyes. I can not reassure you of Aleister's conscious control of his imagination's potential. Irrespective of finding a discreet and accessible ear, he is likely to exist as a loner. You may approach him with these theories, but it's likely he already understands the strength and the persuasive authority of his mind. *In truth he may even bring about his own end.* I do not intend to be dramatic. I only hope I can try and help to explain the situation. The mind is an enigma; there is no handbook; there is no knowing how each of us will operate within its given parameters.

Doctor Tessa Nottingham

I, Professor Giles, have read and understood these complexities and being of sound mind, more the artistic sense than psychological, I leave these clinical notes to accompany the case. I should also like to state, with the compliance of my sister, I offered Aleister her professional card in case he wished to seek help and advice from someone more qualified than myself. She had slipped it into her papers.

Part X

I left this puzzling case for over two weeks. In the meantime I've done some literary research into the queer and curious notion of the mind. A doctor may refer to Aleister and his subconscious in the medical and psychoanalytical sense, labelling the boy with behavioural issues. I wondered if I use the term *creative* or *imaginative* to describe his visions, the whole matter becomes less clinical and more artistic; it is on cultured constructive ground I prefer to stand. This in no way reduces the fearsome ideals of the young boy but certainly puts him in brighter, more optimistic company. It has also given me a new insight to my topic of English Literature. I admire authors as interpreters of their own extraordinary visions, their inventions and their fecundity. The definition itself of imagination fits perfectly with what Aleister creates, *'the action of producing ideas, especially mental images of what is not present or not been experienced; a creative mental ability.'*

This will not take up much time or many pages, but to me it is vital. It presents two cases of Aleister, the doctor's patient and the teacher's pupil.

In my room, top to toe in literature, classical

novels and reference books, where all answers should be found, I stumbled upon a small section on the poet John Keats. I'm versed in his sensuous, symbolic and evocative poetry, with its illustrious use of language, but escape his poetry for a minute and discover the mind of the man himself. He was a great advocate of the authenticity of imagination; he wrote excitedly about it in letters, allowing his thoughts to run away with him, yet if you follow them carefully, as if walking speedily behind someone you wish to catch up, you'll find his argument on the subject a fascinating one. I give a synopsis of a few points of relevant interest. Keats states in a letter to a good friend, '*What the imagination seizes as Beauty must be truth - whether it existed before or not.*' Aleister's thoughts are not beautiful to me but they are to him; he has certainly seized the possibilities of poetical powers and formed them into a real truth. I shuddered when I read also that thoughts are '*a shadow of the reality to come.*' One can be imaginative yet at the same time '*careful of its fruits.*' If we dream of a subject and form it so distinctively in our minds, at some later event it may merge into a truth. These are the private ideas of a man, writing in the early 19th century; by applying them to my present day situation they are as clear and as freshly considered as ever. Might we sit together on the grass as avid philosophers and Romantics discussing maybe even procrastinating on the potential deceitfulness and insidiousness of the intellect and debating both its positive and negative states? The boundaries between these two are so fine as to be almost imperceptible, when they really define two polar extremes.

Leaving Keats and moving to a selection of other writers, I found their statements thought-provoking. Prodded and prompted by printed stimuli, I was tempted to react to and linger on some of their more pertinent phrases. Each time I applied Aleister's story, recalling them to mind over and over, quoting them as I walked Lolly or spent time staring out of the window (a past-time never wasted on me).

The Polish, British nationalist writer, Joseph Conrad wrote, '*only in men's imagination does every truth find an effective and undeniable existence. Imagination, not invention, is the supreme master of art as of life.*' Aleister is creating a life of his own mental making, where he is lead author.

The American writer Ursula Le Guin wrote, '*my imagination makes me human and makes me a fool; it gives me all the world and exiles me from it.'* Aleister lives in two parallel worlds: one real, the other imagined. They both contradict one another, so while we allow our minds to conjure all we wish for, it can make living life intolerable.

The following two quotes almost come with a sharp warning, one from Russian-American novelist Vladmir Nabokov who states, *'imagination, the supreme delight of the immortal and the immature, should be limited. In order to enjoy life we should not enjoy it too much.'* I might ask him: how can you limit imagination? Should we ask the sea to remain constant or a pit to end where we desire? A bottomless pit; vast oceans of inconceivable depths; planets of the galaxy in an unquantifiable space; they are not limited, they are incalculable. The mind and its imagination should be included as one such phenomenon. It's also true, on observation, Aleister does not fully enjoy life; with a mind as productive as his, it is very likely to afflict him.

Then there is a line from Dante, *'imagination, that does so abstract us, that we are not aware, not even when a thousand trumpets sound about our ears.'* Dante uses the word *'abstract'* in the Latin definition to mean, *'remove'* or *'extract.'* Why this is so true! It's as if he had written a short line just on Aleister. The boy is entirely removed from society and natural integration by his imagination. He only thinks, breathes and lives with nothing else but what is stirring in his mind. He will continue blinded and indifferent until his demons achieve full fruition.

I must end this short list of quotes with two British writers. In no way do they reassure me of a healthy outcome for this young man, more of a strong sense of foreboding for his future. Sir Arthur Conan-Doyle, a man of spiritual mystery, wrote *'where there is no imagination, there is no horror.'* Somehow the negating of the words *'imagination'* and *'horror'* make for more ominous overtones.

'People can die of mere imagination,' spoke 14th century writer Geoffrey Chaucer, a most succinct prophesy for Aleister's demonic plight.

Frankly I must confess how tired and low I am from this whole affair. I thought it might lift my spirits but I feel weak and nauseous. Therefore very feebly I end this section.

...

My how time has flown - eight complete months of the same, straight-forward, regimental pattern; no surprises, no mishaps. I even managed to squeeze in a short extracurricular module on Keats and his letter writing after a regional interest in his correspondence came to light. I had become rather engrossed in the topic, whilst researching and analysing some of the new material I was simultaneously able to teach it. For a Professor this is an added bonus, enhancing a subject with up to date discoveries.

Over the last term, as tests and examinations brought increased pressure, I paid particular attention to Aleister whose behaviour over the school year seemed to improve. He socialised with the other boys, though I know he is covering up a darker side; there are lurking elements of a shadowy someone else. How I wished him clean of it. After all, I have seen his split personality in action, befriending and amusing others, whilst harbouring a much more evil inner self. On occasion I felt compelled and obliged to offer guidance and support, but it seems that after the one night in November he has closed off all personal connections with me. Perhaps he feels embarrassed. I refuse to proclaim misleading words, but his lack of communication has left me in a quandary.

He achieved his degree methodically, leaving in June, returning to collect a certificate and attend the annual end of year photo, which sharpened up many of the boys. Somehow I believe I'll never see Aleister again.

Over the long summer period which was dry and dusty I talked a little to my wife of Aleister and to my son who was living at home. However, ashamedly, I omitted too many details and in the end I had made up an entirely new story. Feeling foolish in the process I just let it calmly pass by. Lolly's sprightly sparkle and appetite for adventure kept us occupied. I bought new books and visited many old houses and open homes; trailed the city heritage walks, thereby ticking off my summer must-do list. It was during the long, tedious month of August, whose days were drained by unquenchable inactivity, my son practised his interview techniques on me and prepared his job applications for various charitable organisations. His sensibilities and genuine sincerity kept me relaxed and reassured of his future.

I did not make the summer trip to see my sister. She was unsurprised. I was disappointed. The gap between us widened again; it would be all my doing to shorten it. In this last year I have aged; my voice is gravelly, my body sore, my limbs ache and squeak like rusty doors and my movements more pronounced. As I prepare to take up the next school year I detect I sit somewhat differently in my study chair. It feels as if the universe has shifted its position in the realm (which of course it has) and my alignment on Earth is ill-configured.

A further five years have elapsed. My time as teacher and confidante is drawing to a close; I'd already prolonged my retirement. In my final year, Mrs Lewis (my secretary) organised a former Alumnae gathering. Many old faces returned, but not Aleister. Few of the boys remembered him, not even Mrs Lewis could recollect him, *"maybe the name,"* she said, tapping her chin, *"but not the face."* I found her a highly unreliable source. There was one young boy who must have been three years below Aleister, he portrayed a student of Aleister's description as having *"an 'I'm going to kill you face',"* and *"the waft of the devil about him."*

I conclude I've become rather light-headed and heavy handed about the place. The name, *Aleister Stratton*, has become a tiresome haunt, synonymous with headaches. I see it everywhere, I cannot delete it. It has been impressed onto my memory and I cannot expunge it. All I can do is sit with it day after day, circulating around my head as a dizzy ring of Saturn. I've tried to throw it off, only to feel its unrelenting re-emergence as a pressure upon my temple. I have written this story as honestly and as thoroughly as I feel capable, for me it is over. I leave it to you reader, teacher, lecturer, companion to continue what has not ended.

Part XI

Professor Holland sank heavily into his chair. He sighed and drew breath; the ease of this involuntarily movement forgotten during the course of reading. He wiped his forehead and flushed cheeks; hot tears fell from his grey eyelashes and splashed onto the papers below with a surprisingly loud, definitive reverberation. He had a dumbfounded expression, perplexed wrinkles and his white hands, with pounding blue veins, thumped to the rhythm of guilt-by-association. As of yet Holland remained oblivious to the cause of Aleister's *'unexplained death'* but he knew he held the answer. It was encoded in this story, with integrity and faithfulness. Holland was the recipient of this unfinished tale. He'd chosen to walk its jagged path; an added observer to the case. *His* will and judgment would determine the story's final result.

The tapping rain had imperceptibly ceased; discarded drops slid vertically down the window collecting into puddles. The sun was pulling on what strength it could muster to burn through the clouds and dry up their mess. All life could feel the sun's sense of urgency as it intensified its resolve to warm the earth, promising optimistic rays of sanity and safety. Several minutes elapsed before Holland considered the time and his part in the day. Two hours had skipped past since his reading; there was a further hour before his first class. To return his head to the present situation would take a good mug of coffee and a couple of ginger thins; he fumbled and flustered, preparing both. On the desk he placed the day's obituary page to his left and Professor Giles' papers to his right; his eyes flitted back and forth between the two whilst sipping a bitter coffee and dipping the skinny biscuits, which disintegrated upon entry into the piping hot liquid. This was of no bother to him. Within a short while he was on the phone to the London police number. After passing through a maze of mis-directions, he arrived at the correct department. A concise and practical conversation followed, during which Professor Holland made clear he had some information about the deceased: *Aleister Stratton*. He chose the option of attending the station to make a formal account, ignoring the hint of coercion, concluding it to be the better way to proceed. It was only three stops on the nearest tube line and he would have to make excuses for missing his class. He compiled an outline of work for the students to read and research, and made apologies to one or two members of staff, stating unequivocally, *"a matter of urgent business had arisen and he needed at least two hours leave to deal with it."* Mrs Wallace kindly said she would sit with the class; the simple instructions for the students were undemanding and she understood his dilemma wholeheartedly. He worried she may have known too much; this was surely impossible. His hyper-sensitive, theatrical nerves were playing on him. He did feel anxious and apprehensive yet simultaneously exhilarated, like a school boy chasing a cricket ball; his back, normally sore, eased into the activity and his stooped appearance, straightened, giving back years to the 65 year old. Holland returned to the study to collect his papers. Before entering the room, he stopped and scanned the place as if he'd never looked at it in its entirety; the little office of someone else. He viewed, from the steps Aleister would have taken before approaching Professor Giles, the rack of well-thumbed books, the desk, and the doorway with a completely new set of eyes.

Suddenly there came yelps and shouts from outside, propelling Holland into the study and immediately to the window to witness whatever commotion had alerted him. No matter how we may feel, some movements are performed automatically; this was one. Down below shrill students were splashing carelessly in the newly-formed pools of water; the penetrating sun had given them access to the outdoors and their free-time activity was boisterous and garrulous.

Standing by the window, Holland forgot all about the childish behaviour, and thought only of Aleister. How he had gazed directly on that self-same window view of the world, perhaps mindful of the confession he would deliver Professor Giles, and then with great seriousness and consideration Aleister aired the oddest statement about *'being high up'* and *'breaking your neck.'*

'Yes it was a long drop to the ground' thought Professor Holland. He wouldn't have considered such a prime position overlooking this landscaped scene in the same way as Aleister. This marked the great difference between them. One may see a gardener's fork as a useful tool for weeding; another may see it as a sufficient implement for a murderous attack – in which case we are surrounded by weapons all the time as methods of annihilation. Professor Holland clasped his shaky hands, his spine tickled. He had to get on, he had to focus and he had to move cautiously.

With a swift, rallying movement of his legs, he

spun round, collected his belongings with great care yet celerity, and shot out of the study. There were questions he needed answered, primarily *'what was the cause of Aleister's early death?'* If the police could provide this information, it was likely that Professor Holland could help *explain* their bafflement. As the first tube stop came into view, he had gained time (a rarity) to relax and recharge his mind and mingle amongst the rest of the time-pressured public.

The police station was an intimidating, red-brick building reminiscent of an Edwardian town hall. A War Memorial and two harshly trimmed plain trees announced the front entrance. Sadly the interior had a modern, perfunctory feel with a corporate waiting room and a series of sterile, stainless steel doors running along the corridor, opening and closing like heart valves. Up and down, every space was efficiently busy. Everyone had a task to accomplish; even the rugged and unsightly were performing duties as worker bees in a hive, ordered and uniformed. After filling out a form with a list of personal details, Holland was soon ushered down the long corridor with a series of locked doors each about 8 feet apart on either side. To soften their drabness and homogeneity each room had been named after a British tree, Holland was shown into Silver Birch. He sat down on a hard chair. The walls were painted concrete grey. The door opened and hissing on its regulated hinges, introduced Chief Inspector Warren. He was an amiable-looking man with a deep line running across his forehead, unintentionally directing you to his enormous ears. Holland thought he'd have been happier if the gentleman had appeared dour and stern, after all this was not a picnic jaunt, this was '*an unexplained death.*'

"*Mr Holland, glad you could come,*" croaked Warren, "*we've been waiting for you to get in contact. The boys said I should visit you this afternoon, but you beat me to it... better you did make your own way here, than us coming round and searching through your rooms!*"

"*You've been waiting for me?*" Holland gulped his words.

"*We, I mean I, thought once you spotted the appeal in the paper you'd have something you wanted to share. I'm not alone in solving this case of Aleister Stratton's curious death, but we've been led to you...a Mr, oh no, apologies, A Professor Holland of Regent's College in London.*" Warren said in a lively tone and reading from a scratchy notepad.

Professor Holland took a sip of water, which had materialised without obvious origin, and which he drank with relish. Whether it had been placed on the table for him or not, he felt queasy and needed some cool water to refresh himself. It tasted like the dull walls, grim and bleached. Since this conversation of few words had begun, he could only deduce, there was a much bigger picture being painted, and there were many artists involved in making it come together.

Warren spoke directly now, *"We can speak truthfully and confidentially in here Professor Holland. I don't like to get too formal, it's a terrible deterrent. This is my nephew, Peter."* He pointed to a rotund man seemingly in his late twenties; it was difficult to judge his age exactly. Holding paper and pen and a recording device, he nodded a straightforward hello.

"He's going to take notes, but don't worry, this is part of any procedure, just focus on accuracy...fact, that's all."

He continued, *"I'm not being clear, and you look worried, rest assured, if you have what we've been told you have, then you're the key to resolving this incident. Aleister Stratton was found dead by his sister, Sarah; his neck was broken from a fall, and yet he was lying comfortably in bed. There are no suspicious circumstances, the room and flat have been searched but I'll come to details later. I don't want to alarm you Professor Holland, but I might put the question to you or to anyone, as we've been doing in the last 24 hours: how does a man, fast asleep in bed, die of a broken neck?"* Warren looked at Holland intensely; gentle, weaving interrogation was his skill. He then moved his eyes around the room, acknowledging Peter, who was scrupulously penning and taping everything. *"In this place we're always searching people for honesty and truth, you're not guilty of anything, except, perhaps, of possessing some papers or written material and..."*

Holland interrupted the Chief Inspector before he pressed too seriously. Holland preferred the amicable man to the stern and humourless expression which was fast-overtaking Warren's fleshy countenance. Now Holland had discovered the cause of death, the story he had read was beginning to make sense. It was not perfectly clear and resolute to him, but he was several steps ahead of solving this mystery and before long they would all settle on an answer. Whether they could believe it would require a forfeit of any logical or cohesive thought-process.

Professor Holland spoke with a wide mouth and bright, open eyes. *"Yes, I have brought with me some papers I found and read only this morning."* Although he was uncomfortable, he refused to fidget, he needed to talk; this is what he had come to do. Whilst he held their attention, he would simply run through what had brought him to the station and then, if feeling confident, *he* would do some asking. He sat motionless and prepared.

"I read the name, Aleister Stratton, as an addendum to the obituary page of this morning's newspaper. It sounded familiar to me. I could not, for the life of me, wonder why. Then it dawned on me. When I first arrived at the college 20 odd years ago, I'd been left the previous occupant's three essential and dedicated books: The Bible, an Encyclopaedia and a dictionary. It was inside the Collins English dictionary I found a clump of loose papers. I re-assembled them, they'd got out of order, I read the name Aleister Stratton and the name of his Professor, Professor Giles." Holland took a deep, disguised breath to maintain his composure and to continue his flow re-invigorated. He spoke with fluency and eloquence. The story was foremost in his thoughts and he would not miss out one word, *"I've read the story and I've brought it with me, as you told me I would. You, of course, may take it and*

use it, but I might save you some time. Now I know how Aleister died, I can, perhaps, help explain or decipher your mystery by using this account." Holland held the papers firmly aloft, as if he'd received a trophy. *"But first, how did you know I would come? Who have you spoken to?"* Holland queried. Warren looked triumphant; this was the best piece of intelligent interaction he'd uncovered in days. He was an old dog tracking a scent. He'd need patience with Holland; a man with an interpretative brain and source of potential enlightenment. However, before tolerating the Professor's justifiable questions, the detective outlined the case.

"Well we might as well begin with what we know." Warren emphasised the *'we'* for purpose of group solidarity; he knew it was primarily his probe. He was chief examiner and he spoke with authority.

"As I previously stated, Aleister's sister Sarah, four years older than he, discovered the body two days ago. She is a quietly spoken spinster with a pale and delicate complexion. It took her some time to talk. She was visibly upset and weak, suffering as she did from a chronic shortness of breath. She attributed this to an asthmatic condition developed, she knew not why, many years earlier. When she

breathed to speak her voice took on the tone of a confessional: 'My father died in the same mysterious way,'" Warren imitated, and resumed softly, in the light feminine manner, reading his notes, *"'he was found in bed with a broken neck. For family decency our doctor pronounced cause of death to be a heart attack. A helpful, if duplicitous diagnosis for what he strongly believed to be suicide. The whole affair was illogical and confusing. My mother felt so ashamed and mystified. Their marriage had always been the coming together of two ill-suited people who shared little more than child bearing relations. As a family we never discussed his death. You can never entirely know a person.'"*

Warren watched Holland lean against the table for support. The Professor was both stunned and fascinated in equal measure; so many incongruous events; pieces of a puzzle starting to fit together; the impossible now becoming a truth, but to what conclusion?

Warren continued his narrative:
"Aleister's flat was a neat small studio with few artefacts or personal belongings. He possessed very little. At first we thought he lived elsewhere, but his sister knew only of this residence; located at the top of a central London Art Deco building, a cosy, double aspect room. It looked down on the affluence

of nearby Mayfair clubs with such superiority, even the pigeons roosted two floors below."

Warren tapped his ears in a nonchalant but studied fashion; a gesture he had used successfully over the years to maintain the atmosphere and concentration of his audience.

"Several things come essentially to mind. First, a week old ticket stub to Hastings from Charing Cross, can't say I've been myself, but Jim says it's a pretty sort of town, good for kids and fishing. There were chalky deposits found on his jacket and a sticky, crusty mud stuck to his shoes. We ran some tests on the material and turns out they're found only in the south east of the country, tying up perfectly with a visit to Hastings. Then on his mantelpiece Peter picked up a business card, a Dr Nottingham, it said. Not much else but a phone number with the code for Hastings on it. It looked a bit dated and tired as if it been sitting inside a damp pocket for years. So I phoned the number of course."

Professor Holland almost fell off his chair in expectancy. "For goodness sake," he said, "don't stop there." There was a meditative pause in which time Warren grew in glorious self-satisfaction as he focused on Holland's receptive and expressive countenance.

Warren progressed. "There was no reply of course,

no answering machine, some Doctor, I thought, not doing his service much good. I tried a second time and still the long ringtone. I was ready to hang up when I heard the release of the receiver and a squeaky, 'hello?' I must have sounded like a giant in return! It was a shaky-sounding old lady. I explained the purpose of my call and emitted the necessary apologies for disturbing her this late afternoon. I find myself doing this increasingly as witnesses become older and feebler. It always seems unfair to draw them into these unpleasant circumstances when they themselves don't have long to go. Her faint and muffled speech was difficult to make out. Peter, you have there what Dr Nottingham said." Warren was gesticulating with energy at Peter who was able to pin point the precise phrase Warren was circling his brain to retrieve.

Peter, the man of writing and recording, had not said a word. At first Holland thought this was how Warren liked it. He was in charge and it was his case and his small team; the resourcefulness and abilities stemmed from him. Then he realised that Peter could not actually speak at all. He was a proficient and exemplary speed writer and most importantly, right and left hand man to his uncle, Warren. Peter found the quote and Warren read it slowly for impact, *"'I've not heard the name Aleister Stratton for over*

20 years and no, I have never seen the boy. My late brother, Professor Giles at Regent's College, central London, once spoke of him to me and I made my report on the basis of what I was told. You say he is dead?'" Warren wrinkled his brow, the deep line plunged deeper; he read on, *"'something has been done then, he has brought it upon himself. The only person who'll hold any information on Aleister Stratton and his 'unexplained death' will be Professor Hollerd, no Holland, the incumbent of my late brother's study rooms. He will surely explain it; quite simple it is too.'"* Warren handed the notepad back to Peter.

"After that," said Warren, *"she hung up and disconnected her phone. We could have had a team of people at her door, but I decided to take the opportunity to subtly publish the death in the paper and wait for you to come forward. Ha! I was right to do so and right to wait! What do you say? I couldn't hassle an old lady for more information, I'd have had two deaths on my hands."*

Professor Holland, whose heavy head turned methodically back and forth between Warren and his scrupulously accurate note-taker. He wondered if this was his time to congratulate Warren on his methods or to clear up the case of Stratton in a simple paragraph. By reading through the pages and picking up the hints, clues and complex meanings detailed in Professor Giles' collection of documents and by talking to Warren and learning of his research, Holland's conclusion on the case of Aleister Stratton's *'unexplained death'* was at last cemented. He blew a puff of air from his lungs. He knew Warren would not like the illogical outcome; he was man of fact and hard evidence. Professors Giles and Holland were men of imaginative beliefs; an absolute quality that had bound them from the start.

Holland cleared his throat. He prepared his voice and his soul for the forthcoming release; a release and deliverance to lift his shoulders and lighten his conscience. *"Let me first state that I am entirely well, level-headed and grounded, if a little tired from this whole affair."* Warren circled his hands as if to encourage Holland to speak. Without constraint or concealment, Holland spoke freely:

"Aleister Stratton's neck is broken because he jumped from a great height, perhaps from a cliff or a high window. We'll never know exactly what he chose as his point of death, but I am taking these as two probable options. This is what I have understood by reading all these papers. Aleister suffered terribly

from extremely vivid and intense dreams, call them nightmares if you wish; a term too simplistic. The personal deep-seated misery they devised in his head bred an indivisible state between waking and sleeping. Dantesque in his hell." Holland continued at a pace; he watched the beads of sweat build across Warren's forehead forming into hot-peppered patches. Neither Warren's twitches and irritations, or Peter's bold, brown-eyed stare would distract him.

"You see, what he experienced mentally a few days ago, was conceived so forcibly, it propelled itself into a reality. It pushed through his subconscious imparting his own improbable death. As you say 'how can you die of a broken neck while lying in bed?' This is, and can only be, the explanation. This is what Dr Nottingham discovered 20 years ago and alluded to in her papers. Aleister believed he'd murdered his sister and mother using poison, an action he'd only dreamt. The undertaking was so meticulous and graphic; it felt as real to him as the solid truth. When he discovered they were both still alive, he realised he'd not dreamt deep enough to have achieved the full effect. The mother and sister suffered blisters and shortness of breath. He knew something had been done, but not as he thought. You see Warren, you have been searching out a logical, practical answer, but there is no such answer to give. This is no ordinary case, because this is no ordinary *man. I once read 'the powerful possibilities of our subconscious are frightening. How safe are our minds, for we are all capable of being murderers...'"*

It was now Warren who began to tire. He thought he had heard everything. Here was a contrived plot being read to him. *'Poison?'* *'Blisters?'* He needed time to pore over these detailed papers, these varied accounts. Holland was a decent, trustworthy man; his considered explanation was unrealistic. Chief Inspector Warren *could never* believe or accept it. This case would be left open for years to come. Professor Holland would return to his world to continue daily life independently. Aleister Stratton's case would niggle at the Inspector's brain, knot his stomach, and infect his approach to future investigations until he retired or even longer.

There was nothing more Professor Holland could provide. He handed over the collection of papers, the meaning of which would remain impenetrable to every questioning resource of Warren's career.

He did not once turn back. The dryness on his tongue and the smell of sour yeast from a nearby bakery gave him a dizzy head. He was hungry and thirsty and desperate to return to his study. The combination of all three made his movements swift and keen. Within an untroubled, unruffled half an hour he was climbing the steep and uneven staircase; pouring a glass of Madeira and unwrapping a packet of his favourite savoury biscuits. The bells struck 5 o'clock in the courtyard.

'*Heavens!*' Holland cried. The whole day felt like one of incomprehensible but possible meanings, depending on the configuration of *your* mind.

Part XII

Holland was soon overcome by drowsiness; his eyelids became heavy as if two paperweights were lowered upon them. He did not resist and the closing of his eyes plunged him into darkness. He could feel his heart pumping from the tip of his cold, dry toes to his drumming ears. The engulfing blackness and obscurity made him fully aware of his body. He counted his fingers, he pushed back his hair, he lifted his knee and before he could raise his hand to his nose, to sense the warm air, flowing in and out, he drifted off into a peaceful slumber.

"Professor Holland, it's me, are you there, hello?" came a concerned cry from outside the Professor's door. Several delicate yet urgent knocks had preceded the question.

"Oh, oh, yes I'm here, Mrs Wallace is it? I'm just... er... give me a minute," exclaimed a dizzy and disorientated Holland.

"Sorry to disturb you, it's coming up to 7.30 and I just wanted to go over today's schedule before classes and, well, are you alright? Your wife has called three times this morning; she said you may have slept over again? And...then..."

"Half a second, I'm just coming..." called out Holland.

He appeared at the door. Mrs Wallace let out a tight exclamation, covered it quickly with a cough, which led to a sneeze, thankfully lightening the atmosphere between them.

"Yes, I appear to have slept right through. I surprise myself sometimes!" Holland took one of his customary deep breaths, the first of the morning. He pulled himself round and shook his head, his jumbled thoughts needed re-arranging. *"Let's begin, shall we? "Please, read your list."* He paced up and down the room, exercising his muscles and loosening his limbs.

Mrs Wallace held a deep-creased brow, symbolising a permanent state of worry. She only ever exhibited two faces: one very smiley, dimpled-cheek expression and the afore-mentioned concerned if somewhat bemused forehead, with the nod of the head she could alternate between the two.

"Your wife has called here three times this morning, please get in touch with her." She related this piece of news as if it was the first time she had asserted it, making particular emphasis on

returning the call.

She continued: *"I have just spoken to a Chief Inspector Warren, who says he is sending over some papers you kindly lent yesterday afternoon. He thanks you for their use and... well that was all he said..."* Mrs Wallace, who likes to make perfect sense out of everything, looked enquiringly and sympathetically at Holland's pale and dishevelled state. He was drained of all answers and tired of the querulous stare he seemed to attract from onlookers.

"May I have a tea with two sugars, Mrs Wallace, is there milk? If not I'll have it black, I need lifting," spoke the parched Holland.

"Yes, of course I'll get it now, it's exactly what you need. You have a good ten minutes before the new student interview begins, he'll be here at eight." Mrs Wallace averted her eyes downwards and left to her wrist, reading her watch four times in the space of a few seconds. She couldn't quite grasp today's difficulties and it was still only ten minutes to eight in the morning.

"A new student? I'd forgotten," said Holland, first raising his voice and then lowering it.

"All the students admire you Sir, I'm sure one more young boy to influence and encourage will not harm you! I have his name here and will send him up when he arrives. Now that tea!" Mrs Wallace smiled, she could see colour blending into the Professor's face with every blink of her eye; a bit of active, constructive dialogue did wonders for him, she thought, and while on a happy note she cried from the stairwell, *"His name is Aleister Stratton."*

Professor Holland, beginning his day's contemplation from the window, stood motionless. The soft pinks trying so wilfully to ignite a sense of well being into his face instantly retreated; he turned paper-white with shock. *"That's impossible!"* He yelled and after a set of indecipherable, confusing mumbles, *"I won't see him up in this study, Mrs Wallace. I'll come downstairs to the small front room instead."*

And to himself quietly, *'It's too high up here to trust the course of fate.'* Professor Holland had to act on his already worn and fractured wits. Nothing made sense: *'Chief Inspector Warren existed, so did the account left by Professor Giles and so did Aleister Stratton? The man was dead, wasn't he? Yes to each of these. So who is this new Aleister Stratton? Questions, questions, always questions!*

Let's meet this boy, who calls himself Aleister Stratton and let him do the talking.'

Professor Holland sat in the small, front room, staring at the escaping steam, rising and swirling up the vacant sides of the china mug and condensing into tiny drops, diluting his milky tea, like streams washed up by rivers. After a few minutes the steam died down, and he attempted a couple of short sips. On the table sat the papers, **'The Case of Aleister Stratton by his teacher Professor Giles.'** Had it really only been twenty four hours since turning the pages of this account, sifting through a story of extraordinary consequences? His stomach filled with emotion and then twisted like a spun towel. He placed the handful of papers into the drawer, patting the corners neatly together. There was a gentle murmur outside his door and then a confident knock of three.

Holland raised his head like a curious cat and dramatically cried out the line, *"Come in, Aleister!"*

A neat, young man walked in and closed the door firmly behind him.

"Hello Professor Holland, sir, I'm Aleister Stratton."

Aleister leant forward eagerly to shake,

with practised performance, the thin bony fingers of Holland, who watched every movement and gesture of this charming boy with his fascinating dark blue eyes, his wavy hair and bewitching self-esteem. Holland reassured himself; he was no fool and would not be coerced by sorcery or a trickster.

"Take a seat, tell me why you're here, tell me something of yourself," spoke Holland without an ounce of begging or anticipation in his tone. He held back his true feelings for fear of the boy's retraction, like tapping the snail before he exposes his full body from the safety of his shell.

"Thank you sir. My uncle Aleister came to Regent's College twenty years ago. He's my dad's brother, they weren't close but he and I got on really well. I'd like to study here, just like he did. He told me wonderful things about this place, how much he'd learnt, his great teachers, the old buildings..." The boy was enthusiastic and unfazed.

"Your uncle, you say, Aleister Stratton, very well...I'm sorry to hear of his recent passing..." interrupted Holland.

"Yes it was sudden, he wasn't always well when we did see him...but my dad refuses to talk to me about it. I'd like to be here at this college and work in the same rooms as him. He took English Literature and I'd like to do History of Art. My uncle had great ambitions as a young man, he longed to be a

writer... a story teller. I think he was disappointed he never had his work published or performed."

Professor Holland drank some of his tepid tea; tapping his fingers against the smooth, white ceramic, he said, *"a story teller, you say, did you hear any of his tales?"*

"Yes! Some he'd tell at Christmas, others whenever we met up, which was not often, but he always had a story, a wonderful story to tell me. My dad, aunt and grandmother rarely listened, but I loved it! I feel I've been a child for too long. I'd like to move on with my studies and become something my uncle was unable to be! Please don't think me pretentious, just eager to make a mark on the world where my uncle failed. I feel more his son than my father's." Aleister continued in the same full, bottomless breath brought on by youthful fervour. *"My uncle said Professor Giles was the only one in the world he trusted. There's a lack of paternal interest in our family...anyway he said he'd written one of his most exciting stories here, at this college and had told it and given it to his Professor."*

Professor Holland found himself yet again leaning on his intelligence to understand what exactly was being presented to him. These stories were they *'wonderful'* or were they wicked? He was undecided. The boy's eloquent rhetoric and verbosity caused a pang of pain to his head. Was the tale written by the *dead* Aleister, and handed to Professor Giles, sitting tidily inside the desk, real or a fabrication: a pompous riddle? Professor Giles had believed in its truth; he had continued the story, but was it on false pretences? Was it all just an invention...fiction...fable... forgery...lie? For goodness sake the whole family could be a mythical creation. If the imagination can be dangerous then a living lie can only be its earthly representative. Aleister Stratton has played enough games with us all.

The young Aleister looked so innocent and fresh, so genuinely enthralled. He would be a joy to teach, his excitement could be tamed. With good direction and attention he could achieve his *dreams*. Holland did not like his own turn of phrase. He knew he would have to detach himself from the past Aleister if he was to allow the future Aleister to flourish.

"Return here tomorrow at 8.30, take the list of stationery items and the books you'll require for this term. Take a little time now to familiarise yourself with the grounds and we'll see you tomorrow."

Aleister leapt from his seat, *"thank you, sir! I will, I shall...thank you..."*

Professor Holland opened the door and showed Aleister out via Mrs Wallace's large reception desk. She handed the new student

a list of recommended articles. Holland made a sharp turn; his eyes went wide and bulbous, *"what's this box doing here, Mrs Wallace?"*
It was obvious what it contained but he needed to hear it reasoned. *"Oh, we have rats in the basement again,"* she pronounced, dejectedly. *"This is the poison you have to put down for the beasts. It's a white powder, all the instructions are in there, I'll do it shortly. Apparently they move around mostly at night, oooouuu such a horrid thought. They'll be dead by morning when pest control is due. Don't worry yourself; I've got it under control."* She smiled and lifted her shoulders; her sign of proficiency and capability.
"Goodbye sir, see you tomorrow.
Rats, imagine that!" said Aleister.

Professor Holland looked quizzical; the boy was composed. There was an impish, mischievous echo to his voice. The modulations seemed altered as if infected with a new, mature, fearless note. The affectation was so marked and the look of the boy was so stirring. His eyes, the colour of sweet candied fruit, now appeared acidic, as if you had taken, at first, a seemingly tasty bite only to discover the bitterness of the peel in the aftertaste. Holland felt a cold slice of air run through him, cutting his sense into irretrievable fragments.

During the short interview had Aleister cast a deliberate, false display of courteous amiability? Holland felt sick and uneasy. He put his hand to his hot cheek, let the heat seep into his palm, and wandered distractedly back to the small front room. How dim and bleak it seemed; how burdened and frail he felt. His head throbbed and his eyeballs felt gritty. He went to the drawer, took out the papers and he skimmed through the pages. There was only one thing he could think to do, in memory of Professor Giles, a man he had never known but with whom he felt great empathy. Holland went calmly to the door, *"Mrs Wallace, please ring my wife tell her I've gone to the publishers on Foyle Street! I have something of great interest to share with them."*

With that firm statement penetrating his mind, a curving smile broke his face, as sunbeams part the clouds. A complete change came upon him; a light warmth radiated from his soul. How long this ephemeral pleasure lasted was immaterial; however transitory or fleeting, the future rewards may prove greater than the burdens. He placed the account into an empty file, gripped it surely and stepped out onto the doorstep, seizing a broad breath of good, clean air.

'I shall present **'The Case of Aleister Stratton by his teacher Professor Giles'** to the public, let them read the story, let them decide on truth, on fiction.' He spoke quietly to his inner self, every aspect of his body waking and moving in unified satisfaction. There is sufficient resolution to this case. 'Imagination can be a ruthless tool. The sins of the subconscious creation finally come together and make judgement on the chosen day of retribution. The mind concludes the hour of their reckoning and death collects.'